GET THE AUDIOBOOK

I0536324

*jljarvis.com/*knight-errant

ALSO BY J.L. JARVIS

Waterfront Summers

(Can be read in any order)

The Cottage at Peregrine Cove

The House on Serenity Lake

Moonlight on Mariner's Bluff

Drake & Wilde Mysteries

(Reading Order)

1 Love in the Time of Pumpkins

2 Secrets in the Hollow

3 Shadow of the Horseman

Standalones

(Can be read in any order)

A Cowboy Kind of Love

A Christmas Eve Stop

Christmas by Lamplight

A Kiss in the Rain

App-ily Ever After

Once Upon a Winter

The Red Rose

Highland Vow

Short Stories

Highland Passage

(Can be read in any order)

Highland Passage

Knight Errant

Lost Bride

Highland Soldiers

1 The Enemy

2 The Betrayal

3 The Return

4 The Wanderer

American Hearts

(Can be read in any order)

Secret Hearts

Forbidden Hearts

Runaway Hearts

For more information, visit jljarvis.com.

Get monthly book news at news.jljarvis.com.

KNIGHT ERRANT

KNIGHT ERRANT
A HIGHLAND PASSAGE NOVEL

J.L. JARVIS

KNIGHT ERRANT
A Highland Passage Novel

Copyright © 2015 J.L. Jarvis

Published by Bookbinder Press
bookbinderpress.com

ISBN (paperback) 978-0-9906476-5-2
ISBN (hardcover) 978-1-942767-69-5
ISBN (ebook) 978-0-9906476-4-5
ISBN (audiobook) 978-1-942767-32-9

CHAPTER 1
THE HOMECOMING

Present Day, Putnam County, NY

"Do me a favor and burn the sheets when you're done." Violet Quinn stood in the doorway, too stunned to move.

The couple in bed bolted upright. The young woman clutched the sheet to her chest while the man locked eyes with Violet.

"I thought you were coming home later," he said.

She glanced at the woman. Disheveled brown hair. Pretty. Then she fixed her attention on Jack. His eyes were dark with self-pity. At first all Violet could manage to do was to absorb the shock and resulting nausea without sinking to the floor in a heap.

But from somewhere deep inside, she found strength enough to form words and express them with a dignity she did not feel. "I got done early and thought I'd surprise you." She smiled. "Nailed it. As did you."

Dignity was way overrated. She turned to leave.

"Violet, wait—"

He started to get up, but she stopped him with one pained stare. "Good-bye, Jack."

By the time he had reached for his jeans and pulled them on, she was gone, and he gave up the chase at the doorway.

"Agh!" she groaned when she got outside.

Jack's car was blocking hers. He had dropped her at the airport and planned on picking her up, which at the time, she had thought was so thoughtful of him. How sweet. She now realized he had merely been making sure she wouldn't arrive home to spoil his fun. But an early flight and a car service had foiled those plans. And now she was trapped. Violet looked at the garage. She did have her road bike. She didn't typically wear a silk tunic, leggings, and flats to go riding, but then again, she didn't usually find her boyfriend in bed—her bed—with another woman so... what the heck. This was as good a riding outfit as any. So off she went on her bike, down the winding country road.

She deserved better. She was done with the Jacks of the world. No, she was done with the men of the world! Maybe it was time to take that vacation to Scotland she'd always dreamed about. She could rent a cottage on an island—like that remote one with the whirlpool that sucks boats into oblivion. That would be perfect. She could pack light. The one-way ticket would be a big money saver.

As Violet made a right turn, the idea took root. What better time to get away. Far removed from the distractions of everyday life, she could reconsider her life choices. And cry.

A drop of rain fell on her forehead, then another fell on her nose. "Oh, great."

Then the sky opened to release a deluge.

She glanced up, her tears mixing with raindrops. "Really?"

Lightning answered, followed two seconds later by thunder. The sky took on an ominous greenish hue, and she knew that she had to seek shelter. She glanced back toward her house. No, she wouldn't go back there. Around the next bend in the road was a stone chamber— one of the mysterious structures scattered about Putnam County, NY, for reasons no one quite knew. There were all sorts of theories, some paranormal—not that she was the sort to buy into such far-fetched ideas. No, she was in the camp of those who thought the stacked stone enclo- sures were simply root cellars erected by settlers, though others claimed they were too old for that. Either way, this one would shelter her from the rain that would soak her if she didn't find cover soon.

Propping her bike against the stone chamber's entrance, she went farther back, past a puddle, and sat on a rock. Only then did she let herself cry, and she did a fine job of it—cursing included. She loved him, or thought she did, until she saw him from the doorway, ass bobbing under the Egyptian cotton duvet. They'd bought that bed together when Jack moved in. He had swept her from her orderly life into a rush of passion that, damn him, still made her breathless to recall. Now she would have to take that magnificent bed to the carting company for disposal. How could she have let herself trust him? She had fallen too fast and was now paying the price. Taken in by Jack's good looks and charm, she had made a huge error in judgment. She wouldn't let that happen again. Next time—no, there wouldn't be a next time. She was finished with men. Too tired to think, she just cried. Elbows on bent knees, she buried her face in her hands and just let it all out.

A loud boom shook the ground as lightning arced from the stone wall to the wet ground. Then everything went black.

VIOLET LAY STILL as light birdsong interrupted the silence. She opened her eyes just a crack, as though one move might break her. When she mustered the courage, she moved gingerly. Fingers and toes first then hands, arms, and ankles. Everything seemed to work. As she did so, the image flashed through her mind of the violent surge that had gone through her body. She must have been struck by lightning. What else could it have been? And why not, when the day had been so utterly perfect already? Why break the momentum?

Feeling shaky, she sat up and took in the sight beyond the stone chamber, which looked, from the inside, much larger now. Outside, a river flowed past in sharply cut angles as glints of bright morning sun flickered against the pale coursing water. Beyond, the land stretched out in a soft upward slope to meet the thick woodlands beyond. None of it looked the least bit familiar.

Violet forced herself up and went to the opening of the chamber to retrieve her bike, which she'd left propped against the outside wall. With a gasp, she stopped short and looked down. Where the heck was the ground? The stone chamber now opened to what looked like the side of a cliff. She flattened her back against the wall of the cave until her head and stomach stopped whirling. Breathing in deep, measured breaths, she forced herself to calm down.

"Okay. Okay, so the ground's opened up. An earthquake? But what about that flash of lightning? It doesn't matter. I just need to find a way home." She looked about, still not quite her logical self. If there had been an earthquake, she needed to get out before an aftershock followed.

Violet had long ago tried to conquer her fear of heights. She had mastered the rock-climbing wall on a cruise ship a few years before. Once after that, she had started to climb the Shawangunk Ridge. But the Gunks were steep. She didn't have much of a death wish, so she wimped out. She lost a boyfriend over that. He was looking for a woman who would go on mountain-climbing adventures with him, and she wasn't that girl. His cute climber's ass notwithstanding, it wasn't meant to be. They were from two different worlds, hers being on the ground. Oh, well, just another in a series of failed could-have-been loves.

Violet inched her way to the edge and looked out. "It's not totally vertical. And that might be a path."

Her stomach sank as she contemplated the climb. It wasn't quite as steep as the cruise ship rock-climbing wall, and she had climbed that more than once—well, just twice. But she had been harnessed to a rope to catch her if she fell.

"You can do this." *I'm going to die.*

Violet stepped out of the cave. She found a foothold

and a tree branch to hang onto. She could do this. One foot after the other. No big deal. But the distance to the ground below was a big deal, and a dizzying one. Violet carefully made her way down, foothold by foothold, taking time out to hug the cliff face until a moment of panic subsided.

She held on and pressed her face to the stone. "I usually get taken to dinner before this much full-frontal contact."

When she summoned the courage to take the next step, a rock moved under her foot. She gasped and held on by the tips of her fingers.

"Hold on," said a male voice.

"That's the plan." She clung to the rock, too afraid to move to see who had spoken.

A moment passed. "Are you all right, mistress?"

Too terrified to move, she said, "I've been better."

"Give me your hand." His rich voice sounded sure.

"I would love to, but I'd have to let go."

When she didn't reach for him, he moved closer and put his hand over hers. His touch, strong and warm, made her feel safe—the same way Jack's touch used to do. The image of him in her bed with that woman flashed before her, but she willed it away.

"Take my hand."

His quiet confidence brought her back to her current predicament. He gently eased his fingers about her hand until she grasped his hand. She glanced to her side, and soft gray eyes met hers. Deep set and calm, those were the eyes of a man she could trust—with her life, anyway. Not with her heart. She would never again trust a man with her heart.

The path widened in front of some foliage that grew from a fissure. He guided her there then talked her down, step-by-step, handhold-by-handhold until they arrived at the ground, where she flung her arms about his neck and clung to him, trembling and too relieved to be on terra firma and in a sturdy embrace to think of anything else. He held her securely until her heart stopped hammering and her breathing grew steady. Then his arms stiffened, and he stepped back.

"I'm sorry!" Violet stepped back and held her palms toward him, doing her best to regain her composure. She shook her head and, with a feeble smile, met his eyes. He looked awfully concerned—for her sanity, no doubt. "I'm so sorry. I kind of lost it there for a minute. It was nothing —just the terror. I'm fine now. Thank you."

His troubled demeanor gave way to a courteous bow. "Robert de Mallay, at your service."

She took the bow well, but when he lifted her hand and kissed it, her knees buckled. She blamed that on not having had anything to eat since her airplane pretzel breakfast. "Violet Quinn."

Her hand twitched from the reflex to shake hands, but he already held her hand—right below his mouth. He lowered her hand and released it on its own recognizance —his assumption surely being that she wouldn't reach for his collar and pull him against her to see if his lips felt as good on her mouth as they had on her hand. That was the bitterness talking. What better way to vent her anger with Jack than by proving that she didn't need him by throwing herself at the next guy who talked her down off a ledge?

"Mistress Quinn, may I escort you somewhere?"

Violet looked quizzically at him. To say he was strange was the least of it. He sounded Scottish, which wasn't all that unusual. After all, people traveled. But he was wearing what looked like a doublet, trunk hose, and over-the-knee leather boots. It wasn't a bad look, actually. It gave him a sort of Elizabethan punk rock vibe that was a far cry from the khaki and pale pinpoint-oxford palette preferred by the men who peppered her typical day. But still, something wasn't quite right. They were only an hour away from New York City. With as much time as she spent in the city, how had she missed this new fashion? Oh, well, what did she know? It wasn't as though she spent her days in the Garment District. She was an accountant in her company's White Plains office. When she went to the city, it was usually to take in a play. The theater district had far more tourists than New Yorkers, so she had clearly just missed a new fashion trend. She made a mental note to pick up a couple of magazines to catch up.

As for his hair, it was long and unkempt—whipped by the wind. She wanted to smooth it back down, every last brown-black strand, because underneath all that hair were gray eyes that were gentle and warm—and still staring at her. She nearly apologized again but stopped herself. *Don't make it worse.* Yet how could it be any worse? She'd already found her boyfriend in bed with someone else, had a panic attack on the face of a cliff, and now she was alone with a strangely dressed man—and all before lunch. Although, he had just saved her life, and he was—if she were interested in that sort of thing at the moment, which she was not—striking, in a tall, dark, and brooding way.

"Where are you bound? I will see you there safely." He grasped the reins of a horse tethered nearby—a horse that she had failed to notice while fixating on him. How had she not noticed a horse?

"Well, I seem to be lost. If you would just point me in the direction of Farmers Mills Road?"

"Farmers Mills—" He squinted and looked off to the distance.

"Road. Yes."

He shrugged. "I'm sorry. I dinnae ken where that is."

He glanced about, and Violet followed suit. Nothing looked as it should. She had grown up in Putnam County, New York. She and her friends had explored most of the hiking paths within thirty miles, so she ought to know where she was. She did not.

"I can take you back into the city, if you like."

"The city? No, thank you, I'm fine. Thanks for rescuing me." She smiled, but it faded under the shade of his stature. Why he fixed his eyes on hers, she didn't understand—but she didn't complain, either. If she were in need of a rebound guy, he would do. But she wasn't. No, that was the last thing that she needed. What she needed was to go home, spend some time alone, and plan a restful vacation.

Just as she was getting used to his gaze, he looked away. "Well, I'll not leave you here."

"Why not?"

"Because it wouldnae be right." Without asking again, he took her hand and guided her toward the horse.

Violet wasn't one to take orders, nor had he given any. He seemed to assume she would ride with him. Violet took stock. What choice did she have? She was lost and on foot, while he had a horse and he knew where he was. The stone chamber was near Fahnestock Park, so there was a good chance she was lost somewhere in its sixteen thousand acres of state parkland. So her choices were to wander alone and wind up eating bugs and the wrong kinds of plants for survival, only to die or, best-case scenario, vomit her entrails out—or she could allow a stranger to take her to safety. That was her most sensible option. He had done nothing but help her. Not only did she feel safe with him, but he had an uncanny way of making whatever he said seem like the right thing to do. She wouldn't call what she felt trust—because Jack had ruined that for her—but since Robert had brought her to safety, she supposed she could defer to his judgment this once. So she climbed onto the horse, then he mounted behind her.

They followed a path by the water, which Violet assumed was one of the many reservoirs in Putnam County that supplied drinking water for New York City. Before long, they rounded a bend, bringing into view a walled city across the water, which she could now see was, in fact, a river. It was too narrow to be the Hudson River. She didn't recognize the location or the stone bridge spanning the water. She looked about and was forced to admit with unsettling certainty that she was, indeed, lost.

He nodded toward the city. "That's Perth."

"Perth?"

They stopped outside the city gate, where he let her down off the horse to go on her way.

He eyed her, frowning for a moment. "Have you someplace to stay?"

Violet gave him a sharp look. "I'll be fine." He hesitated, unconvinced, but she lifted her chin and dismissed him with a curt, "Thank you."

"Very well then." His eyes softened. "I shall bid you farewell."

Violet was already beginning to lose the power to think under his gaze, but when he did that hand-kissing thing again, he finished her off. All she could do was emit a garbled mess of breathlessness that would have to do for a good-bye.

He rode away looking tall and sinewy—just how she liked them. Just like Jack.

"And look how well that worked out," she reminded herself.

She watched him until a third person brushed past her on their way into the city, and she started to walk. *"I shall bid you farewell?" Who says that?*

CHAPTER 2
THE GLEANERS

There was no city named Perth near Violet's home. The only place walled-in like this was the nearby Greenhaven Prison, but this wall was different. Instead of cement, it was made up of stones, like the medieval stone walls she had seen around old castles in Scotland. She fell into step with a stream of people passing through the main gate. Apparently there was some sort of Renaissance Faire going on. She hoped that, once inside, she might find a phone or someone willing to offer directions. She had already asked a few people, but they looked her up and down, crossed themselves, and walked away without saying a word. They could stare all they wanted, but they were the ones who looked as if they had leapt off the canvas of Millet's *The Gleaners*. She shrugged off their reactions and went on her way.

As she walked down the High Street, she had no goal in mind, but she felt sure she would find her way home just by walking until something looked familiar. A low murmur grew to a din as a crowd rounded a corner and moved steadily toward her. It looked as though they were reenacting a mob of angry villagers. All they needed were some torches. She wanted to laugh, but they looked awfully serious—a point that was driven home the closer they came. No, they weren't joking. For reasons she couldn't fathom, they were coming straight for her. She had to get out of their way, so she plastered herself to the wall of a shop, but the mob spanned the street from wall to wall. A door opened, and a firm hand grasped her wrist and yanked her into a shop. The door closed as quickly as it had opened.

With no explanation, she was pulled toward the back of the shop, where a thin ribbon of light from a shuttered window revealed her cliff rescuer. "Robert?"

Looking past her toward the front, he said, "Are you mad?"

"No, I'm lost."

"Aye, that much is clear."

"I thought I'd ask someone for directions."

He eyed her strangely.

"Look, I know it's a foreign concept to men, but I—" A loud thud at the front door startled her into silence.

Robert glanced toward the door but ignored it and returned his gaze to her.

Violet said, "The thing is, I don't know where I am."

He studied her, his brow creased. "Where were you before we met?"

"In the cave."

"And before that?"

Violet met his intense gaze, which made her lose her trust in him, although she couldn't say why. Perhaps it was because Jack had had the same sort of intensity when she first met him. She'd later realized that the riveted look that made women blush was no more than a parlor trick —one that had worked on her.

Instead of answering, she said, "Where were you?"

"I was at the bottom of the hill when I looked up and saw you."

A man called from the rear of the building, "Robert, we'd best leave before it's too late."

Still grasping her wrist, Robert peered deeply into her eyes then turned and led her through the back door of the shop, where a monk waited with two horses.

"Henry, Mistress Quinn is coming with us."

Henry leaned closer to Robert and lowered his voice. "'Tis a bad idea, and you ken it."

"We cannae leave her here alone."

Henry opened his mouth to speak, but seeing Robert's narrowing eyes, he shook his head instead. He glanced toward the creaking front door. It would give way to the crowd before long. "We've no time to argue."

Violet stepped closer to the arguing men. "Excuse me, but shouldn't I have a say?"

Robert met her determined expression with one of his own. "I'll not leave you here. You dinnae even ken where you are."

Before she could answer, the crowd broke through the door.

Robert hoisted her onto his horse. "Here's your choice: if you want to live, come with us. If not, stay here."

The din of the crowd convinced her he might have a point. Henry grumbled about how this would slow them down, but Robert ignored him and leapt up behind Violet.

As they rode, Robert leaned over, scooped up some clothes draped over some bushes to dry, and handed them to Violet. "Hold these."

Violet took them and said, "Why?"

"You can put them on later."

"Why?"

"Look at yourself. Dressed like that, not to mention your strange speech, you'll be tried as a harlot or a witch."

Violet smirked. "Sure, John Proctor." When he failed to share her amusement, she said, "Look, thanks for the ride, but I can walk from here."

"I've no doubt." He made no effort to slow down. They emerged from the wynd ahead of the crowd but just barely, and made it through the Highgate, trailing behind Henry.

"You can let me down now."

His arms remained firmly about her as he leaned down and spoke close to her ear, "You must trust me."

"Last time someone said that, I shouldn't have."

"Did I not get you down the cliff safely?"

"Yes, but this is different."

"Aye, it's more dangerous. Look behind us."

Violet turned to see a crowd on foot heading toward them. "Are they following us?"

"Nay, lass, but they may as well be, for it looks like they're headed where we are."

"And where's that?"

"Ahead, to Blackfriars Monastery." Once there, Robert dismounted and helped Violet down, and he left Henry with the horses. "Stay close, and do as I say."

Robert took Violet's hand and led her to a door where a tall, sturdy monk with graying hair waited for them.

"Brother Thomas, this is Violet."

The monk's gray eyes settled on Violet for only a moment, then he gave Robert a questioning look. He started to speak, but Henry joined them, and Brother Thomas stopped.

Brother Thomas handed Henry a bundle. "John Knox has exhorted his people to cast down the idols of the kirk. I've gathered the most valuable ones here. Take them to the Sinclairs in Roslin for safekeeping." His speech made it clear that he wasn't from Scotland.

Henry nodded and went back outside.

When Henry was gone, Robert said, "Violet has come from the cave."

The two shared a knowing look, and Brother Thomas lifted an archer's quiver. But instead of arrows, it held a rolled up length of linen. Thomas glanced sideways at Violet and spoke cryptically. "We once spoke of how this day might come."

A dark look came into Robert's eyes.

Brother Thomas put the quiver in Robert's hands. "Guard this as you would your own life, for it may be more precious. Its secrets will be lost if you fail in your mission."

Robert nodded gravely and slung the strap diagonally over his chest so the quiver hung over his back alongside his own arrow-filled quiver. He turned to Brother Thomas. "They'll be here soon. Will you not come with us?"

"I've a hidden room here where I'll be safe." The

monk clasped Robert's hand in both of his. "I'll not see you again."

Robert's brow furrowed as he clenched his jaw and reluctantly nodded. "I dinnae ken how to thank you."

"To see the man you've become is enough thanks for me." Brother Thomas gave Robert's shoulder a firm grip then released him.

Robert turned to Violet. "Come, lass."

She started to follow him, but Brother Thomas put his hand on her arm. "Take care of him."

Violet wasn't sure how to respond. She began to protest and explain how things were, but something stopped her. Perhaps it was the warm light in the older man's eyes. "I will," she replied.

As they rode away, Robert said, "He was like a father to me."

Behind them, the mob of reformers arrived and began to loot Blackfriars Monastery.

The three rode in silence until Henry looked back and called to Robert, "Do you see them?"

"Aye."

Violet looked back and saw two horsemen in black gaining on them.

Robert circled her waist and pulled her back against him. "Stay close against me so I can shield you."

"Shield me?"

An arrow flew past them. As Robert urged his horse on, something fell from the bundle tied to Henry's saddle. Henry pulled on the reins.

Robert cried, "What are you doing?"

Henry ignored Robert's cry and went back for a jeweled chalice that had fallen.

Robert wrapped Violet's hand around the hilt of a dirk. "Hold this tightly and be ready to use it."

Violet clung to the saddle as Robert pulled an arrow from his quiver and turned to shoot at the oncoming riders.

"Leave it!" Robert cried to Henry.

Ignoring him, Henry slipped from his horse and grasped hold of the chalice. As he turned to put the chalice back in its sack, an arrow struck him in the back. His back arched as he gripped the saddle, gasping. He turned to face his attackers. With labored breathing, he reached toward them and opened his mouth to say something, but no sound came forth. He drew his sword and made a few feeble swipes and thrusts as the riders overtook him.

Robert leaned over Violet. "Stay down."

She clung, trembling, to the saddle while Robert leapt to the ground, sword in hand. Only then did she notice that the two men wore black priests' cassocks. One came at Robert with a dagger while the other swung a sword and sliced Henry's neck from ear to ear. Violet tried not to gasp as blood sprayed the swordsman.

The two men then leapt onto their horses and rode away, leaving Violet watching them, stunned. A man had just been brutally killed before her. What sort of a world had she come to if that was the norm?

"Are you all right?" Robert asked softly.

She nodded, although she was as far from all right as she had ever been.

"Take Henry's horse."

Violet stared at him in disbelief.

Robert waved her toward the horse. "Go on."

"You want me to ride that?"

Robert sheathed his sword and looked at her. "Aye."

"By myself?"

He drew back, frowning. "Do you not ken how to ride?"

"No." She saw his disappointment.

"You'll catch on."

"No, I won't."

"I can teach you."

Violet shook her head.

Robert studied her for a moment. "First cliffs, now horses; you're a skittish lass, aren't you?"

While she did not appreciate his characterization of her, there wasn't much she could say to rebut it. He left her searching for words and went over to Henry's horse. He said something too quiet to hear and gave it a smack on the rump to send it back toward the friary.

Violet said, "Henry died for those treasures."

"Aye, and that's one person too many. Let them have their bag of trinkets. I'll not die for them, and neither will you." He took her arm and led her to his horse. Without a word, he helped her up then mounted behind her and rode toward the hills.

Violet's head swam for a moment, and she swayed. Robert must have felt it, for he put one arm about her waist and held her against him. He was stable and sure, neither of which she was. Perhaps, for now, it was enough that they were alive and riding into the cool, bracing mist.

CHAPTER 3
CROSS PURPOSES

A small stream wended down a cleft in the hills. They stopped to give the horse water, food, and some rest. Exhausted, Violet drank some water and, in lieu of a highway rest stop, found a tree she could hide behind to take care of her personal needs. After the morning she'd had, what did niceties like plumbing matter?

At this point, she wasn't entirely sure that she wasn't in the midst of some sort of psychotic break. Yes, Jack had hurt her—a lot, truth be told—but was it enough to cause this? Perhaps she was subliminally killing off substitute versions of Jack to internally vent her rage over being betrayed? Violet tended to overthink things.

She returned to the clearing to find Robert's horse contentedly eating, but no Robert in sight. Violet lay down on a patch of soft grass and breathed in its sweet scent. Exhausted, she closed her eyes and blocked out the world. She had always slept well under stress. It was her way of coping. She dozed until the grass stirred beside her.

She opened her eyes to find Robert seated nearby and studying her.

She sat up abruptly and pushed thick brown waves of hair from her face. "How long was I asleep?"

"Not long." He looked away quickly, as though he hadn't been watching her. She started to stand, but he touched her arm to stop her. "Rest. We must bide here for a time." Violet wanted to ask why, but he spoke before she had the chance. "We'll hide here for the night then head south, passing Perth, in the morning."

"Passing Perth?"

"Aye."

"You know, I have been racking my brain trying to think of where that is. Do you mean Perth Amboy? New Jersey?"

He grimaced and gave his head a slight shake. "Scotland."

"Scotland?"

"Aye." He tilted his head and looked at her as if she had lost her mind.

She was inclined to agree with him, for how could that be? Of course she had noticed his Scottish accent, but it wasn't so unusual to hear a variety of accents in the New York area. But there was no Perth in this part of New York, and nothing that she had experienced here could have happened at home.

Even if there were a rational explanation for her being in Scotland, this couldn't be the Scotland she had visited once. She thought back through all she had seen today. Not once had she seen a car or lights. Everyone had been dressed as though they had jumped out of the past—or she had jumped into it. As the idea sank in, Robert met her confused look with a calm she couldn't share. Nor could she find words to make sense of it. She had gone beyond shock and felt numb inside.

Robert said, "There is a story that is told around fires on dark nights about a cave overlooking the river that is known as the Dragon Hole. There a dragon once lived. He terrorized the people below until one day a monk named St. Serf went to slay him. He climbed into the cave and confronted the powerful dragon. Praying to God, he was given the power to slay it. As the dragon died, a stone fell from the dragon's forehead. There it lay in the back of the cave for generations, until one day a man named James Keddie happened upon it. He touched the stone and vanished."

"And your point?" Violet said dryly. When he did not answer, she looked at him. His expression pierced her veneer. She looked away, hoping to hide it.

Robert said, "I've been inside that cave, and it took me to your New York."

"You're as crazy as I am."

"No, I'm not, and neither are you."

Violet shook her head. She wouldn't look at him for fear she might believe him.

He said, "I still long for the pizza."

"Whose pizza?" Violet narrowed her eyes.

"Ray's."

She grinned. Of all the things he might have said, that made as much sense as any. The city was peppered with pizzerias all claiming to be the original Ray's. "But how did you get to New York?"

"'Tis a secret kept by the monks. I cannae say more, for I've taken a vow."

Violet tried not to groan. "You're a monk?"

"I've spent my life preparing to be one."

"Of course you have." Violet hid her disappointment. He would have made such a perfect rebound guy, dammit. How much worse could this day get? "So you've taken a vow to become a monk."

"No, not yet—just a vow of secrecy."

"Well, that sounds very 'tinfoil hat.'" When he failed to react, she said, "Illuminati? Skull and Bones? Knights Templar?"

At the mention of the latter, his eyes widened, but he quickly averted them.

Violet leaned forward. "Get. Out. You are not a Knight Templar!"

"No. I am simply a knight, but my father was a Templar."

"Does that mean you're *Sir* Robert?"

He offered a humble shrug.

"But the Knights Templar disbanded back in—"

"1307," he said without hesitation.

"And it's now—"

"1559." Violet blinked slowly then stared at him until he added, "Today is the eleventh of May in the year of our Lord 1559."

"And we're in—"

"Scotland."

"1559 Scotland." Violet stared toward Perth, unable to fathom what he had just told her.

He looked off into the distance. "My father was a Knight Templar in France. He did many brave and good deeds, but he committed one sin. He fell in love, and the Templars vow to be chaste. The woman he loved was a nun. When the Templars came under attack, my father chose his own penance, but before he did, he saw my mother safely on her way to a megalithic stone structure called a dolmen, which was known to the Templars to have the power to send people through time. With her safely embarked, he faced his accusers. Her journey brought her to the future in Perth, where she found her way to the Blackfriars Monastery. They took her in, and there I grew up."

Violet reached out to touch him but withdrew her hand. "And your father—do you know what happened to him?"

"He was burned at the stake, along with more than fifty others." Sir Robert eventually broke the long silence that followed. "And what of you? How did you find your way here?"

Violet's brow creased. "This morning, I caught an early flight home from a business trip to surprise my boyfriend, but he surprised me. He was in bed with some woman."

"Och, the philandering knave! He's a whoreson fit only for hell." He hastened to add, "Forgive me. I spoke without thinking."

"Oh, believe me, I've called him much worse." She met his eyes and managed a weak smile that was gone the next moment. "So after that, I left and got caught in the rain. I guess I was struck by lightning. And here I am." She took in a deep breath and exhaled with despair. "I just want to go home."

"Aye, lass." His sad gaze somehow comforted her until she suspected that his sympathy was caused by something he was withholding.

She said firmly, "I have to go back."

With a slow nod, he said, "Aye, but we cannae go back there—not now."

Violet wanted to cry. She ached so much that the weight of it kept her tears from flowing. She thought about going alone to the cave—and she would if she had to—but she was afraid of heights. Planes and bridges didn't bother her, but she had never climbed up so high and so close to the edge. One misplaced step could send her tumbling hundreds of feet to her death. So the truth was, she was hoping that Robert would help her as he had before.

With a deep breath, she assumed her usual false air of assurance that always served her well at the office. "You've been more than kind, but there's no reason for you to come with me. I'll manage alone."

He looked into her eyes. "I cannae let you go alone either—not now. But I will see that you get there when it's safe to do so."

His honest gaze lingered for only a moment, but she felt its effect nonetheless. Life in this time was so harsh one moment, with swords cutting through air and flesh. And yet, in the next moment, people—well, Robert— reached out with a desire to help her that both warmed her and made her uncomfortable. She had trust issues. She could thank Jack for that.

Robert turned away and looked quietly over the city below and the fields beyond. Violet followed his gaze. Setting aside everything that had happened today—and that was a lot—she felt a moment of peace. Robert's calm strength and confidence made her feel as though she could afford a moment or two to regroup.

He glanced at her. "I ken how you must feel, for when I traveled to your time, I had to fend for myself. It was exciting, confusing, and sometimes fearsome. I would not wish that on you."

"More fearsome than having a man coming at you with a sword?"

"Ah, I understand swords, but your world was so different. Simply crossing the street was a life-threatening ordeal. There were dangers there far worse than swords."

Violet thought of him wandering through parts of Manhattan. Dressed as he was, he would have been quite a target.

Robert said, "If you had been there with me, I would have trusted you."

Violet thought about what it would have been like if she had known him then. She would have stayed close beside him to explain things he wouldn't understand. She lifted her eyes, and those gray eyes drew her in.

"Now I am here with you. Please allow me to keep you safe from harm," he said.

He didn't look as though he was trying to persuade her for his own purposes. That was what troubled her. Was he honestly making an offer of help out of kindness? She couldn't fully believe that.

Violet said, "All I want is to go home and curl up on the couch with a book—and maybe a glass of wine—and a fire in the fireplace. I just want to feel safe."

"And I want that for you."

Damn, if he didn't have a gift for making her want to trust him. But that was her weakness. As smart as she was, she believed the best about people. Yet only that morning, she'd had yet another reminder that people didn't always deserve her faith. She shook her head but could form no more words.

To her surprise, he got up and left her. He just walked into the thicket of trees and leaned his back against a trunk. After she accepted the fact that the conversation was over, she got up and walked in the other direction, which happened to be toward the city. Oh, she got it. Message received. He had made an offer of help out of duty, and now that duty was discharged. She was on her own. She didn't fault him. She had pushed her luck to the limit. In fact, she respected him for it. But it was time for her to move on and take care of herself. Yes, she was scared of the climb, but she would scale that wall by sheer will.

"Violet!"

"Don't give in," she said to herself. She had had it with men and emotion. She called, "I'll be fine."

Without looking back, she kept walking away. She expected him to argue the point, for it would have been a good one; she was in no way prepared to go anywhere by herself. But instead, he caught up with her and grabbed her arm with a force that spun her around and into his arms. He held her, first with the same strength she had seen him display when he wielded his sword, then it softened into an embrace, and his hands slipped over her back. One hand cradled her head then moved to her cheek. Violet lifted her face. He stared at her, bewildered, then shifted his weight. He grabbed hold of her shoulders and stepped back.

Feeling a bit disconcerted herself, she looked at him with a nervous smile. "You don't really fit the monk profile, do you?"

He displayed no reaction, except to give her a hard,

lingering look. Abruptly, he took her wrist and pulled her back toward his horse. "We're leaving."

They arrived at the clearing, where he made a noise that drew his horse to him. That impressed Violet.

"Up you go," he said.

"Do you think I'll obey like your horse?"

"No." He looked angry. "Mistress—"

"Violet."

He glanced up, averting his frustration. "I'm trying to help you, but I need you to trust me."

Everything she saw in his gentle gray eyes told her that he was honorable, but she had made that mistake before. "I'm sorry. I can't."

"Violet."

But she did like the sound of her name when he said it.

He took hold of her shoulders. "Listen to me."

Between the sound of her name when he said it and the warmth of his touch, he had her attention. She looked at him with her cool, corporate gaze, but faced with his earnest kindness, her veneer faltered.

He moved closer and spoke with a firm, even tone. "Let me help you."

"What can you do that I can't do for myself?"

"I can guard you with my life, and I will, if you'll let me."

Violet looked down to hide how he had broken through her defenses. Against her better judgment, she found herself trusting him. He lifted her chin. For his trouble, she managed a blank stare.

He spoke in a hushed tone. "Violet."

How did he do that? Simply by saying her name, he

made her heart skip a beat. And her eyes were now stinging with tears. *Oh, great—cry, why don't you. That'll teach him.*

When he failed to continue, she did her best to sound impatient. "What?"

He leaned so close that she felt his warm breath on her cheek. "Will you allow me to help you?"

Violet lifted her eyes and looked squarely at him. With a sigh, she said, "Okay."

He registered a fleeting moment of surprise at her acquiescence then nodded. "Good."

Violet gave a firm nod but averted her eyes. Despite her best efforts, each time their eyes met, she felt as though he caught a glimpse of her heart, and that heart was too vulnerable right now to be glimpsed. For all of his talk about protecting her from his world, who would protect her from him?

The rest of the evening was taken up with a supper of bread and bannocks he had brought with him. He wouldn't light a fire, lest they be discovered, so they ate in cold silence.

Unable to bear it any longer, Violet said, "So you visited New York in my time?"

"Aye."

She waited, but he offered no more. "And ate pizza. What else did you do?"

"Two policemen stopped to talk with me. Someone, it seems, had seen me walk by and, for some reason, found my sword threatening, even though it was sheathed."

Violet smiled. "So they called the police. Did they take you to jail?"

"No, but they did take my sword. Then they took me

to a place called a shelter. It was run by a kirk, and they let me stay there and work."

"For how long?"

Robert shrugged and combed his fingers through his hair. "Och, I dinnae ken. More than a fortnight, I believe."

Violet leaned closer. "What made you return to your own time?"

"I went to a library."

Violet smiled to imagine what a first visit to the library must have been like.

"Aye. I found a book there about Scotland that foretold the future—my future, your history. When I read what would happen in my time, I had to come back."

Violet wished she had been a better history student. "What happened?"

"You lived part of it today. John Knox is leading the country into a religious reformation. And because of what happened today, there's something I must do."

Violet was curious, so when he didn't elaborate, she said, "Well? What is it?"

Robert looked at the city with a faraway look in his eyes. Torn from his thoughts, he shook his head. "I cannae tell you."

"Because then you'd have to kill me?"

Robert looked insulted. "What sort of man do you think I am?"

She laughed and patted his arm. "I was joking!" She thought she saw him flinch when she touched him, but it was so slight, she decided that she had imagined it. "Does it have something to do with those priests who attacked us?"

He took a moment to consider. "Perhaps. I cannae help but wonder if Henry had something to do with what happened today."

Violet studied him. "But they were priests."

"Aye, priests who want something I've got." He shrugged off the thought. "Dinnae fear, lass. I'll keep you safe."

The fierce resolve in his eyes convinced her that he would. "Okay." She couldn't help but wonder over his dogged concern for her welfare, yet she had seen just how brutal a place this could be. Her typical response to stress was to make light of it, but his Scotland would prove her undoing. Although she had tried to block it out, visions of Henry's death flashed before her like a series of horrific still images.

Abruptly, Robert got up and went to his horse. "We'd best get some sleep."

He had one blanket, and he gave it to her. Violet offered to share it.

He looked sternly at her and said, "No, it wouldnae be proper."

"It's just a blanket. I wasn't offering to share anything else." Violet's annoyance was lost in the gray twilight mist.

"Good night." With that, Robert walked a good dozen paces away—no doubt to avoid her dreaded womanly wiles—and lay down and slept almost immediately.

She grew to resent that over the next several hours, when sleep didn't come as easily to her. As she lay awake, thoughts of Jack came back to haunt her. *Six months of my life wasted.* She had seen signs that things weren't right, but she had dismissed them as nothing to worry about because that was what she wanted to believe. The late nights "working," the hushed phone calls he told her were business. Women hovered like moths about him, and he made no pretense of not noticing them. With the flash of his smile or a glance, they were dazzled—as Violet had been. At the same time, he had grown more demanding of her, claiming she didn't love him. Nothing she gave him was ever enough, but she tried with what love she could offer.

The whole thing between them had flared up so fast, and from the start, it was thrilling and hot. But even back then, he confused her. She'd tamped down her doubts and gone on because she thought they were falling in love. All relationships went through the strain of learning about one another and finding out how to make two lives work in sync. She thought they would find their way through. When her business trip came, she was partly relieved for the break. It gave her time to think and conclude that some changes were needed. Still, she believed they could work it all out. And then she came home.

For all of his fire and passion, Jack's heart was a shell made of ashes. One touch, and it crumbled to dust, leaving her feeling bitter and used—and yet wiser. She now knew the difference between lust and love.

"So that happened," she whispered to herself. "But it won't happen ever again."

All she wanted was to be home. She longed to curl up in a blanket on her bed—no, on her sofa. She wouldn't touch that bed. She would order a new bed, and when it was delivered, she would pay the delivery men whatever it took to make that old bed disappear. So back to her sofa.

She would curl up with her favorite down pillow and cry —which she couldn't seem to do now.

A snort startled her. Was Sir Robert snoring? Violet smiled. Well, so much for Prince—or Sir, rather—Charming. Talk about tragic flaws. And his nose was a little bit crooked—probably broken in battle while gallantly wielding a weapon against some villainous foe. She smiled yet again. What was it about him that made her do that— and a little too often? She sighed. There was no use in wondering, because she would be leaving for home at her next opportunity—which was when? She could see Perth from here, and she knew where the cave was. In spite of his chivalrous offer of help, she could be home much sooner if she went back to the cave on her own. Why tag along after Robert on his noble knight's mission, or whatever it was he seemed bound to do before he would take her to the cave? He could save mankind without her. Sure, the climb would be rough, thanks to her fear of heights. It's an irrational fear, she reminded herself. Yet it seemed natural enough, when the cave was hundreds of feet above the ground, to feel certain reluctance toward going from one to the other. She took a breath and exhaled. *If this is what I have to do to go home, then I'll do it.*

Violet stood and set out for the cave. She thought of the dress Robert had, well, stolen for her. For an instant, she thought about going back for it, but even if she managed to get it without waking Robert, the thick folds of fabric would hinder her climbing. After that, she would have no need of it. It was dark anyway. No one would see her. So she continued, leaving behind the gown. And Robert.

CHAPTER 4
A MATTER OF CHIVALRY

Robert opened his eyes. At first he thought Violet was going a discreet distance away to relieve herself, but the footsteps continued. Wincing, he sat up and wearily watched her, the full moon lighting her way. A moment passed as he thought about letting her go. She had become a distraction from the mission he had sworn to fulfill. Yet he had promised to protect her, and he was a man of honor—not that she cared about that. She wanted no help. That much was clear. But she had no idea what hazards loomed for her.

Minutes later, he was on horseback, taking his time descending toward the city. There was no need to hurry. He knew where she was going, and he could still see her shadowy figure in the moonlight. Dressed in her modern attire, she was certain to draw notice. Who else would look after her, let alone understand her, as he could? He was duty-bound to keep safe this young woman from the future. This very appealing young woman, thought the monk. Would-be monk.

In truth, Robert had struggled for years over women —or rather, the prospect of living without them. Raised in a monastery, he had experienced no other life but that of a monk. Until left for battle, he had known little of the world outside the friary. When he had walked among women at market, he had stolen glances and admired their soft skin and womanly curves. He wondered just how those curves would feel to his fingers or pressed against him. He had wondered so much that he frequently took to his knees out of penance. But it did not stop him. That was the one thing that made him doubt whether he could ever vow to be a chaste monk. Still, they were doing God's work, and he had been chosen to carry it on. That was why he was there, they told him. And Robert strove to be worthy.

One spring evening, he had happened to see Brother Thomas emerge from a crypt under the chapel. He carried what looked like a portion of a human skeleton in his hand. Curious, Robert followed him into the workshop where Brother Thomas attended to the holy treasures and relics. Robert watched through a crack between the door hinges as Brother Thomas placed the bone inside a silver reliquary lined with red satin. As the monk turned to leave, Robert stepped behind a pillar. Brother Thomas's robe swished as he passed by.

The following Sunday, Brother Thomas presented the reliquary and its contents—a so-called ancient bone from a saint—to a wealthy benefactor. Robert didn't hear the name of the saint. All he heard was Brother Thomas's lie ringing in his ears. He left the chapel early and went into the city, away from the lies. Until then Robert had sinned without intent, and it was followed by nagging remorse.

But the monks he had always looked up to had deliberately lied without shame. Their lives, Robert's included, were built on those lies, trading false relics for true riches, and all in God's name. Feeling betrayed, his faith shaken, Robert ran away.

Tall, strapping lad that he was, it wasn't long before he found work in a tavern. There he came to know all about life—and the tavern keeper's daughter. On the first day, he set down a cask, and she smiled at him with a warmth that distracted him from his chores. On the second day, he smiled back. On the third day, she taught him the ways of the world on a bed of fresh hay in the loft of the byre. For days after that, they stole burning glances and found moments and places to release their deep longing. It was bliss.

But one morning, the tavern keeper's daughter was gone. She returned in the evening a bride. He had heard talk of a wedding, but not knowing whose, he had paid no heed. All along, she had been promised in marriage to a neighboring shopkeeper—an older man who didn't deserve her. And now she was his. Dressed in a fine gown with rings on her fingers, she caught Robert's gaze for a moment. Then she turned to her husband and gave him the smile that used to be Robert's, and that was the end of it. Robert had once more been betrayed.

The next morning, he returned to Blackfriars.

NOW HE WAS FOLLOWING a woman because he had been fool enough to promise to protect her. And why? Because he was a chivalrous knight? Perhaps, but also because of her soft aqua eyes and thick hair he could tangle his fingers within as he breathed in its scent. He could only imagine how her skin would feel against his on a soft bed of hay—God's wounds! When would he learn?

Having closed the distance between them, he arrived at the bridge that crossed over the River Tay. She was halfway across when two men drew close behind her on either side.

Robert approached her on horseback. "Mistress Quinn."

"Sir Robert!" She looked surprised to see him, but she seemed even more startled to find that two men had joined her.

The taller one gripped her arm. "Step aside, sir. We are taking this indecorous wench to the tollbooth, where she belongs."

"For what?" Violet tried to yank her arm free, but the shorter one grabbed her other arm and held on.

"I'm afraid you're mistaken." With one sweeping motion, Robert extended his sword until it touched the taller man's neck.

The man's companion pulled out a dirk, which Robert intercepted with his foot. His kick made the dirk fly into the water, nicking the short man's cheek on the way. He cried out, holding his face. The taller man thrust his dirk forward, but Robert turned just in time to slice through the man's sleeve and leave a gash in his arm.

As he cried out, Robert pulled Violet onto his horse. "Hold on."

Violet did just that as they rode back over the bridge and around the city wall. Across the river from Kinnoull

Hill, Violet said, "You can let me off here. I'll swim across if I have to."

Making no effort to slow down, Robert looked over his shoulder. "I cannae let you do that. The river will catch you in its current and sweep you away with the tide."

"I just want to go home."

"Aye, but I cannae let you go until I can see you there safely."

She tried to sound calm. "I appreciate all that you've done. Look, I'll even put on that dress you got me, and I'll blend right in crossing the bridge. But I'm going home."

"Aye, but you'll come with me first. When I'm able, I'll bring you back and help you get safely back to the cave."

"Thanks, but I'd rather not wait." Without waiting for him to reply, she slid off the back of the horse.

Robert reached for her and grasped her arm, but her momentum pulled them both to the ground. "Och, woman!"

She got up and ran toward the city. He caught up with her and hooked his arm about her waist just before she reached the town wall.

Violet struggled. "Why won't you just leave me alone?" She shoved her elbow into his waist.

He let out a slight grunt, but his grip didn't weaken. He spoke close to her ear. "Calm down, lass, or you'll draw attention that won't help either of us."

"I don't care."

The more she thrashed, the tighter his arms clamped around her. "Och, careful now. I dinnae want to hurt you."

"But you will if you have to?" she said accusingly.

"That's not what I meant."

"So much for chivalry." She tried to turn around to look at him, but he held her too tightly.

He spoke calmly. "So far you've done more hurting than I. You've a formidable elbow."

She fell silent.

"Violet?" He leaned over her shoulder to look at her face, but she turned away.

A slight sniff followed another.

"Och, lass, dinnae cry." He tenderly turned her about, and she buried her face in his chest, softly weeping.

Then she punched him in the stomach. She cursed and muttered something about his six-pack as she ran away.

Robert rolled his eyes and ran after her. Catching up, he grabbed her and spun her around. She tried to wriggle free, but he pulled her against him and held on until she gave up the struggle and met his annoyed glare with stubborn defiance. He answered with a glower. Her eyes widened then flitted downward. He usually reserved such looks for men with sharp weapons pointed at him, but he had had enough of her. She had disrupted his plans and defied his instructions with little regard for the consequences, not to mention his inconvenience. Moreover, a stray spiral of hair had fallen over her brow. It was driving him mad, so he moved it away from her eyes, which reflected the moonlight. Then he was lost. She glanced down, and he followed her gaze only as far as her lips, which were pouting—no doubt to bedevil him. He leaned closer, unable to help it. Nothing mattered except putting his lips on hers.

She lifted her eyes. "You were right."

God's teeth, was there no plan this woman could not thwart? "About what?" He did not bother to mask his impatience.

She shook her head. "I should have listened to you."

"Violet..."

"No, I've made everything worse. But don't think that means you can boss me around, 'cause you—"

Robert kissed her mid-sentence.

"Can't," she whispered.

He kissed her again.

Voices drew nearer. Robert looked toward the city gate and exhaled.

He took her hand and led her to his horse. "We must leave now." He helped her into the saddle then swung himself into the saddle behind her. "Are you all right, lass?"

"Yes." Her voice had an edge.

Robert started to ask if something was wrong, but she wasn't elbowing, punching, or trying to run for the cave, so he raised a brow and rode on through the dawn mist in silence.

AFTER AN HOUR OF RIDING, Violet opened her eyes with a start.

"'Tis all right, lass. You dozed off."

She wrinkled her nose and looked about at the farmland with crops newly sprouting from its rich soil. An old sandstone bridge crossed the river before them. "Where are we?"

"That's the Brig of Earn."

Violet murmured a sleepy response and nestled back against his chest. Robert caught himself smiling and refocused his thoughts. Halfway over the bridge, a loud banging sound came from behind them and startled his horse, causing it to rear. Robert gripped the reins with one hand while he reached for his sword with the other. The sudden motion tossed Violet sideways. She lost her grip on the saddle and fell to the ground. A hoof narrowly missed her as she rolled out of its way and pulled herself to her feet. Robert subdued his horse while two riders approached, one from each end of the bridge. Both wore black Jesuit cassocks and wielded swords, like their attackers outside of Perth.

As one headed for Robert, Violet went at the other with her dirk. With a shout, the priest swept his sword behind his back in a swift circle and thrust it toward her, stopping a hair's breadth from her chest. Then he struck her dirk with the flat edge of his sword and sent her only weapon flying into the river. With a fleeting glance, as though she weren't threat enough to warrant the effort, he turned toward Robert, who thrust his sword and nicked the first attacker just under the left eye. His eyes flashed, but he quickly recovered. The second man joined in, ignoring Violet, who stood on the side of the bridge.

A moment later, a rock struck the first horseman's head. Robert glanced over to see Violet grab the priest's leg and, despite his kicks, manage to pull him from his horse. When he tried to get back on his feet, she leapt, hands reaching for his throat. He scooped his hands upward between hers and pushed her hands in opposite directions. A knife-like jab of his hand to her throat sent her to the ground, coughing and gasping. Retrieving his sword, he went after Robert, whose attention was on the first priest. He had just knocked the sword from the first priest's hand when the second priest swung at Robert's neck. Robert ducked just in time to avoid it and thrust his own sword into the man's chest.

A strong hand pulled Robert's leg from the opposite stirrup. As he turned, the first priest flipped him in an arc from his horse to the ground. Robert pushed up off of the ground, but with balletic grace, the priest swung his foot at Robert's elbow and sent him falling once more. A sword slid along the ground toward Robert's hand, and he caught it. Eyes blazing, Violet pulled herself up. *The lass has mettle.*

The priest spun around and almost floated as he leaped toward Violet, but Robert lunged and thrust his sword. It glanced off the priest's ankle enough to make him fall short of his target. He pulled himself up, but before he had regained his balance, Robert rushed at him, yanked him up by the throat, and pushed him over the edge of the bridge. The wind fanned out the priest's hair as he fell, grotesquely framing his blood-splattered face. Dark, chilling eyes glared up as he landed, back first, in the water. The next instant, the current swept him away.

A flash of light reflecting off metal caught Robert's eye, and he turned to find a dirk heading for his chest. Robert blocked the move with a strike that barely slowed the man down. Robert's sword and dirk lay scattered somewhere on the ground, lost in the struggle. He had only his bare hands to fight against the dirk being thrust at him. But the man froze, and the dirk fell from his hand. A moment later, his body went limp and crumpled, a dagger sunk into his back.

Violet stared at the dead man, her bloodied hands palm up before her. "He was going to kill you."

Robert pulled her into his arms. "Braw lass."

He held her until she stopped trembling, then he took her hands and gently wiped off the blood with his cape. When she didn't react, he circled his arms about her and held her, stroking her hair. After Violet pulled away gently, he turned and bent to pull the dirk from the attacker's back.

After wiping it on his cape, he offered the dirk to Violet. "This is yours now. You've earned it."

She took it, but rather than showing the pride he hoped she'd feel, her knees buckled. He caught her and held her securely.

Lifting her chin, he said, "You saved my life."

She nodded but said nothing.

By mid-afternoon, they had made their way safely to shelter within the dense woodlands. Too weary to go farther, they stopped to rest for the night.

In the warmth of the afternoon sun, Violet stared at the fire and tried to make sense of the day. To save Robert, she had gone against everything she believed. She had taken a life. Who was she to choose one life in exchange for another? A life for a death—she had made the choice in an instant, and now her hands were bloodied. Despite that, her heart suffered no such conflict, for she had saved Robert.

She lay down to rest. Robert covered her with a blanket and lay beside her. His body felt strong and warm against hers. He was all that she needed or wanted right then. They had been to the brink and faced death, and together, they had returned. It connected them somehow, beyond logic or words. If her thoughts wouldn't fall as neatly into place as her heart, then perhaps it was best not to think at all. Warmed by Robert's body, Violet sank into a deep sleep.

Night had fallen when Violet awoke to find Robert roasting a pheasant. As she sat up, he looked at her, and the corner of his mouth turned up. Violet pulled the blanket over her shoulders and clutched it tightly about her. Still groggy, she was content to sit in silence and watch Robert tend to the pheasant.

An unexpected calm that she hadn't known since she had arrived came over her. At some point, her anger with Jack had dissolved. So much had happened to change her perspective. It now seemed so long ago—or rather, so far in the future. It wasn't until all her anger was gone that she realized how strongly she had felt it. She was hurt but not broken, and she would move on. She now realized she had chased an illusion. Jack had been thrilling, all flash and no depth. As time passed, his lack of genuine, unselfish emotions had left her feeling as though something were missing. She had tried to ignore how it weighed upon her, but the truth was, she hadn't been truly happy with him for some time. His recent actions had just forced her to face that. Doing so lifted a burden, and now she felt free.

Then there was Robert, who wanted nothing more than to help her. Why he hadn't left her by the wayside any number of times, she couldn't say. But he hadn't. Instead, he had protected her. And he had kissed her. Of all the things he had done, or might have done, that kiss had opened her eyes. Evidently the road to Damascus ran southward from Perth. In that instant, she had realized that all of her resistance to Robert's advice had been fueled by anger and pain, all of which was Jack's fault. What she did with it now would be hers. She had given into fear and been overwhelmed by the strange surroundings that fueled her desire to go home. But Jack, the man who had hurt her, was there, while here was Robert, kind and brave—and protective of her. In a place where hostility flared up with no warning, there was something to be said for his protection. No matter what happened, Robert would look out for her. She couldn't say the same for Jack. In that moment, the power shifted, but that was the problem. Now it was Robert whose actions would affect her, for he held the power to guide her home or break her heart—perhaps both.

He brought her some pheasant meat stuck on a stick. "Are you hungry?"

"Ravenous." She took it and lifted her eyes. "Thank you."

The warmth of his smile shone through his eyes as he sat beside her. While they ate, he talked about what they would do next. First, they were going to Edinburgh.

"What are the inns like?" She knew better than to

hope for five-star hotels. She would settle for clean and free of infestation.

"We'll not be in an inn. We'll stay at the Blackfriars Monastery. It will be safer there."

With that settled, they talked of Robert's journey to the future and what he had thought of her time. Before long, they were laughing, completely at ease with each other. Violet wondered what her life might have been like if she'd met someone like him in her time. But that was the problem—he was a product of his time and circumstances. There would never be anyone like him in her world. When they had finished eating, they went to the stream to wash up.

Violet watched him refill a water skin. "What's that made of?"

He glanced at her with a spark in his eyes. "Sheep bladder."

Violet's expression froze. "Oh."

Robert grinned and got up. Taking her hand, he led her back to the fire. She liked the feel of his hand against hers. They sat by the fire, and he put his arm about her shoulders. A piece of log in the fire broke and sent sparks up into the darkness. Robert put his hand on the nape of Violet's neck and combed his fingers through her hair. Violet tilted her head back into his palm as he leaned closer to breathe in the scent of her hair.

"I have wanted to do this since I first saw you clinging to the side of that mountain," he said.

She would have smiled, but his touch took away her breath. She couldn't think clearly. She could feel though, and that was a problem. Her emotions were raw. All she wanted was to sink into his arms and insulate herself from the harsh world she found herself in, but doing so would expose her to worse upheaval, for Robert was already a presence in her heart. She had not meant for that to happen, but it had. It was too late to guard her heart from him now. All she could hope for was damage control, for the pain he could cause when they parted would only grow worse. She knew that she ought to say something, but what? "Stop, your touch reaches a place in my heart that is wounded, and I want you there?"

Jack's actions faded in the face of something far greater. She didn't want to say it or even think it, but the word was there in her mind. No, this couldn't be love. She couldn't fall in love with him, because her heart would break when they parted. But even if they were parted at that moment, she would feel the loss. And the longing. No matter what happened, there was no hope of coming through this unscathed. So she did what made the least sense of all.

She kissed him.

CHAPTER 5
FOR WANT OF A MAID

R obert had kissed women before, and he had thoroughly enjoyed it, but this kiss was different. While he was taking his time to explore just how different it was, she pulled away.

"What's this? Tears?" He lowered his brow. "And what next, will you clout me?" He smiled.

She glanced at him then cast her eyes downward. "No."

Robert's smiled dissolved. "Violet?"

She gave her head a slight shake, and the words poured out. "I'm sorry. I thought I was ready, but I'm not."

"Ready?" He wanted to say it was only a kiss, but he would have been lying. From the start, he had known that his feelings for her were different from any he had known.

As she turned away to wipe her tears, Violet assumed a practical tone. "Even if I were ready, I'll be going home soon. There's no point in complicating things."

Robert nodded, but he did not agree. She might make sense, but what was life worth without risks? Even so, it was her choice to make, and she clearly had made it. So he wouldn't argue the point. Besides, he had things to do. Feelings for her would just get in the way. "Very well. We'll not complicate things."

Her eyes darted up to meet his, but she looked away quickly. "It's better this way."

With a grunt of agreement, he got up and fetched a blanket for her. "Get some sleep." He tossed the blanket beside her.

AFTER A MORNING of riding on horseback with Violet nestled in his arms, Robert decided he had exercised enough self-control for not only a monk, but he ought to be canonized a saint. He had not once given in to the urge to put his lips, or his hands, anywhere he could reach. But although his conduct had been saintly, his thoughts had not been. He was still a man, after all.

Robert broke a silence that had stretched on for miles. "We must buy you a horse in Edinburgh."

"I can't ride. I've told you that."

"I could teach you."

Violet's voice sounded strained. "I don't want to learn."

"But why?"

"I fell once, okay? And that fall on the bridge didn't help either." She sounded as though she was losing her patience. "Look, this was all your idea. I didn't want to come, so it's really not fair to blame me for tagging along."

That was the last thing on his mind. Robert's eyes trailed down the soft slope of her neck to her shoulders, and he shook his head. Tantalus had nothing on him. Up ahead was a burn where they would stop to water his horse and put Robert anywhere but within reach of Violet.

Once they were stopped, he pulled out the last of the bannocks and offered them to her. When they were both finished eating, he went to his horse and returned with a bundle.

"Put this on." He dropped it beside her then walked away, sounding gruff. "We'll be arriving in Edinburgh this afternoon. You'll need to be properly dressed."

He went to the burn for some water. When he returned, she was gone.

"Violet? Are you all right?" he called.

From behind some brambles, he heard, "I'm fine. Just give me a minute."

Robert stood for a while by the horse, then he walked to a nearby tree and leaned, arms folded, waiting. A long while passed. "Are you almost ready?"

"Making progress." Her voice sounded strained.

Robert sat on a log, growing impatient. When he could stand it no longer, he said, "Come, Violet. We must go now."

Violet slowly emerged, her face flushed with frustration, clutching her bodice about her with one hand in back and two detached sleeves dangling from the other. Her eyes burned with frustration. "How do women get into these?"

Robert shook his head then dragged his hand through his hair. "I'm sorry. I dinnae ken. I suppose they have servants to help them."

"Great. Well, let me know when mine gets here."

Her hair fell in uncombed tangles over her shoulders. The wind caught her skirts, and the bodice was crooked. Robert wanted to smile, but her glaring eyes stopped him.

His eyes betrayed only a hint of amusement. "Would you like me to help you?"

"No." She looked away long enough to roll her eyes. "But I haven't much choice, have I?"

He went to her and turned her around. She had fastened a few of the bodice hooks at the waist, so all he needed to do was fasten the rest, which he started to do. His fingertips brushed her skin, soft as satin. She had no shift on underneath, for he'd taken none for her. His eyes swept over the trail of skin between the rows of unfastened hooks and eyes.

She turned partway around. "Is everything okay back there?"

Brought back from his reverie, he said, "Aye. I'm just trying to—" *Do something other than touch your bare skin.* "I'm trying to line up the hooks with the eyes. Ah, here we are." He worked quickly to fasten her up before he succumbed to an opposite urge. "There." He turned her about. "Now for the sleeves." With those tied in place, he stepped backward to appraise his work.

When he failed to utter a word, Violet gave him a questioning look. "Well?"

With a perfunctory nod, he said, "Fine." She looked beguiling—more so than was good for either of them. "See what you can do with that hair," he muttered as he turned and went to his horse.

"Do with it? Like what?"

He waved his wrist. "Confine it somehow."

He couldn't meet her eyes. They had agreed to keep

their feelings in check, and his clearly were not. He tried
to force his thoughts elsewhere and failed. *The unfastened
bodice. The soft skin inside it.* They would dispose of the
dress as soon as they reached Edinburgh. Not only was it
too enticing on her but it was red, which, under the
sumptuary laws, should only be worn by the upper
classes. Even if he could pass her off as a foreign aristocrat,
as bonny as she looked, she would draw too much attention. They needed to blend in, so that would not do. As
soon as he could, he would get her something else to wear
—something shapeless and drab would be nice. But no
clothing was plain enough to quell what he felt for her at
the moment.

TRUE TO HIS PLAN, their first stop after arriving in
Edinburgh was a shop just off the High Street, where
Robert bought Violet some clothing, complete with
proper undergarments and a bodice that laced up the
front, so she could dress herself without his help. He
could not very well leave her outside while he shopped, so
he told the shopkeeper that Violet was mute to avoid
exposing her telltale modern American speech. He
claimed the clothes were for a servant and was thankful
the shop owner was discreet enough not to ask why he
hadn't sent the servant to fetch her own clothing.

They made their way next to the Blackfriars
Monastery, where they were taken in. A monk escorted
them to rooms they referred to as cells. They had missed
supper but were brought porridge to eat in their cells.
After making quick work of the porridge, Robert lay on

his cot. He was exhausted and hoping to rest, but thoughts of Violet on the other side of the wall interfered with his plans. As dusk settled, a monk came to escort him to vespers. They stopped at Violet's cell, and she emerged dressed in her new peasant clothing of muted earth hues.

When Robert stared for far too long, she touched her shoulders and looked down to smooth out her skirts. "Have I done something wrong? Do I look all right?"

"Aye," he said gruffly and walked away.

"Gee, thanks," she muttered.

Once vespers began, Robert found himself soothed by the music, at home in the familiar routine, until he saw Violet looking at him with a look he couldn't quite decipher. He leaned closer.

"I'm not Catholic," she whispered. "What do I do?"

He leaned close to her ear. "Follow me."

That forced him to be aware of her for the purpose of easing her discomfort, thus increasing his. She watched him and followed his lead, kneeling and standing whenever he did, and when it was over, she touched his arm lightly and thanked him.

After that, they were parted. One monk led her to her cell while another led Robert away. The abbot had summoned him.

THE ABBOT HAD delicate features and a quiet manner that put Robert at ease. A well-traveled man, the abbot now sounded more English than Scottish. He had just offered Robert a seat when a quiet knock at the door interrupted their light conversation. A monk brought in

Robert's quiver containing the scroll and handed it to the abbot, who ignored a sharp look from Robert and turned it over, examining it.

"When I was in Perth, a young nun lived at the Blackfriars Monastery. Sister Claudine." The abbot paused, almost smiling. He looked at Robert and went on. "She worked in the garden, and she would talk with the monks while they worked. One monk, in particular, found himself drawn to her. He supposed she was lonely and needed a friend, which he was glad to be. But when he spied her behind a tree, being sick, he worried. Some days later, on a warm afternoon, she suffered a fainting spell. The monk rushed to her aid. As he helped her up, he put his arms about her waist, and there was no doubt that she was with child. Then she confided in him, telling this story.

"Long ago, in the days of the Templars, a young knight broke his vow to be chaste, and the woman he loved was a nun who had taken a vow of her own. Overcome by their love, they gave in to their desires.

"When King Philip IV rounded up Templars for execution, many scattered. But the knight wouldn't leave his beloved behind, so he stayed with her, risking his life. The other Templars took all of the treasures with them, except for one item. They had overlooked a linen scroll that lay in the chapel behind the altar. It held secrets, that much the knight knew, although he didn't know how to read it. But he knew one thing: the scroll had to be kept from King Philip. To do that, the monk would have to leave and return later to his love.

"Faced with losing her knight, the nun agreed to leave with him and begin a life together. But as they were preparing to flee, the king's men broke in. The knight wouldn't leave without the scroll, so he went back to the altar to retrieve it. He had hidden it inside a quiver to protect it from harm. He was on his way out of the chapel when the king's men saw him and called out. He stopped in the doorway and, unseen, gave the quiver to Sister Claudine.

"'If anything happens to me, keep this safe,' he told her. 'It belongs to the Templars. Return it to them when you're able.'

"The footsteps of the king's men drew near. The knight opened a wooden panel in the wall, revealing a secret passage leading out of the monastery. With haste, he guided her into the passageway. 'Go to the dolmen where we used to meet, and wait for me there.'

"She turned back to him. 'Not without you.'

"He fixed his eyes upon her and closed the passageway panel as the king's men entered the room.

"She did as he told her and went to the dolmen, but he never arrived to join her. One morning, she awoke in the brilliant sunlight to find herself in a cave outside Perth, more than two hundred years later. She found her way to the Blackfriars Monastery in Perth, where she was taken in.

"On a rare cloudless night, stars peppered a sky of black velvet. Nearly lost in their midst was the faint silver curve of the moon. As Sister Claudine looked up and dreamt of the knight she had lost, she felt a twinge of pain, but it left just as quickly. When the pain kept returning, she walked down the corridor and found her friend, the monk. She spoke softly to him. He took her back to her cell. Once there, she showed him the scroll and asked him to keep it safe for her child if anything happened to her. He dismissed her pleas as the ravings of a woman in pain. She made him promise to safeguard the only legacy she had to give to her child. She said if anything threatened the scroll, it was to be taken to Roslin. The Earl of St. Clair would know what to do."

Robert went to the window and looked out while he tamped down his emotions.

The abbot went on. "In the quiet hours before dawn, after the stars in the night sky had faded from view, she gave birth to a son. She did not live to see the sun rise. You know this story?"

With a backward glance toward the abbot, Robert said, "Aye. Brother Thomas has told it to me."

The abbot fixed his eyes on the scroll coiled inside the quiver. "Shortly after your birth, the scroll disappeared. I had not seen it since, until now. It was her wish for us to raise you, which we have done. The Blackfriars have watched over you and will continue to do so. You are not alone."

Robert turned from the window.

"Have you looked at it?" Father Abbot reached inside as though he might remove the scroll, but he glanced up at Robert and stopped.

"Once." Before going on, Robert extended his hand with a questioning look, and the abbot handed the quiver to him. "But I didnae ken what it meant, nor was I ever supposed to. I'm to pass the scroll on. I'm no more than a messenger, really." He met the Abbot's knowing gaze as he slung it over his shoulder. "I'm on my way to deliver it."

"Ah, well, I'll not keep you. May God speed you on your way, lad." He clasped Robert's hand.

"Thank you, Father Abbot."

Once back in his cell, Robert thought of the abbot's story, which he had heard before. But there was more to it than the abbot had told him.

AFTER ROBERT HAD RETURNED from his days of rebellion in Perth, he had confronted Brother Thomas about the false relics, and Thomas admitted to what Robert had seen.

"I am not proud of it, lad, but we need the funds for God's work."

"Could God not provide the funds for you?"

"God gives us the ability to provide for ourselves."

"By lying and cheating?" Robert asked.

"To accomplish God's work."

They argued in circles for the rest of the evening. In the end, Brother Thomas agreed, to a point, but he said it was the way of the world. If they did it to serve God, then what was the harm? But Robert's faith was harmed, and it would never again be the same.

As the months passed, they put their disagreement aside and grew closer again. One day, Robert was helping Thomas dust the relics. When they were finished, Brother Thomas told Robert to sit down. He proceeded to tell Robert a fanciful story about travel through time. He had always told Robert his mother had come from another place and time, but Robert had dismissed it as a tale meant to make a lonely young child feel better.

"For years, people have speculated about the secrets of the Templars, never guessing that the greatest secret had naught to do with treasure or wealth. It was knowledge passed down through the ages." He peered into Robert's eyes. "They knew the secret of traveling through time."

Robert shook his head. It was madness.

"What better way for the Templars to control the world than by being able to travel backward and forward through time? The Templar treasures were the least of it. Think of the power and influence they could exert."

"And the scroll?" asked Robert.

"I don't know all of its secrets, but I believe it could be a sort of map. I believe there must be stone structures scattered in key places throughout the world, and one of those places is the Dragon Hole outside of the city. Your mother appeared there and found her way to us from the year of our Lord 1307."

Robert shook his head. It could not be true. But one morning, when the sun shone brightly, he set out for the cave and soon found himself hundreds of years in the future in a land called New York.

CHAPTER 6
THE SECRET SCROLL

After a night of fitful sleep in the monastery, Violet went to breakfast with the monks. She didn't see Robert there, which left her more disappointed than she cared to admit. After breakfast, she went to his room. When he wasn't there, she grew uneasy and went to the stables. His horse was gone. Growing concerned, she looked about and found a stable boy who couldn't have been older than ten. He admitted that he had seen Robert ride away.

"When?"

"Before dawn, mistress."

Violet looked at the horses with no small amount of fear. Knowing that she would be safe here, he had left her alone. What choice did she have? She could find him, which was highly unlikely, or she could stay and make a life with the monks, which was even less likely. If he didn't return—and she doubted he would—there was no point in lingering here. She would have to ride back to the cave.

"Would you saddle a horse for me, please?" she asked.

With wide eyes, the boy said, "Oh, mistress, I cannae do that."

"Yes, you can, and I need you to do it right now."

He looked down. "I'm sorry. I cannae. He said—"

"Who?"

The boy lifted timid eyes. "Sir Robert. He told me I wasnae to let you near a horse."

"Oh, did he?" That provoked Violet's ire, but she tamped it down, for it wasn't the boy's fault. With forced calm, she said, "Did he say where he was going?"

The boy shook his head. "I'm sorry, mistress. I was mucking the stalls, and he paid me no heed when he left."

She let out a frustrated cry. Robert had left her alone with no assurance that he'd return. The boy's eyes opened wide with distress.

The sight tugged at her heart, for she knew she had caused it. "I'm sorry. What's your name?"

"Will."

She smiled softly. "I'm sorry, Will. You've been very nice, and I haven't. Please forgive me."

A smile bloomed on his face. "Oh, no, mistress. You've no need to be sorry."

"Tell me, did he happen to say anything else?"

"No. Well, I think he said something about coming back tonight." The boy frowned, still trying to remember.

Violet's mouth hung agape at that key bit of information, until she remembered herself and gave him a warm smile. "Thank you, Will."

A monk came around the corner and joined them. "May I help you, mistress?"

Violet shook her head. "No, I was just talking with Will."

The monk nodded. "Well, when you're finished, the lad has work to do."

"Yes, of course. I'm sorry."

The monk turned away, and she made a face that drew a smile from the boy.

She whispered, "Thank you."

"Aye, mistress."

She walked away, thinking only of where he could have gone. If she knew the area, she might be able to catch up with him, but she did not. Nor did she know how to saddle a horse, let alone ride off in search of him. With a sigh, Violet realized there was nothing she could do except wait. He was gone, and she was trapped, forced to wait for him to return—if he returned. For if he felt the need to leave her behind, he might have been expecting some danger. She was safer here, as was he without her—wherever he was. She hated to admit it, but he may have done the wisest thing. Her presence might have prompted him to protect her at the cost of his life.

And so, restless, Violet walked around the monastery grounds then went to her cell. It might have been nice if he had let her know what his plans were. How could he not know she would worry? But then, why should he keep her apprised of his actions? She was the one who had put distance between them. Was it fair to resent him for honoring her wishes? But he was out there somewhere, with the scroll that had some sort of value, and where there was value, there would always be people who wanted it for themselves.

LATE AFTERNOON SUN filtered in through her small window. Violet bolted upright on her cot, disoriented. She had dozed off. The events of the past two days had caught up with her. But what had woken her was a commotion of scraping feet and bumps on the wall from Robert's cell. She was on her way to the door when someone knocked on it. She opened the door to find one of the monks with an urgent expression.

"I've been sent to fetch you," he said.

She followed him next door to find Robert on the cot, leaning back against the wall and barely conscious.

"What's happened?" Violet rushed toward him, but the monk who had fetched her held her back.

A second monk held Robert while he vomited into a pail. "He was attacked riding out of the city."

"It was only a scratch," Robert protested.

"Aye, but your skin's cool and clammy, and your heart's racing." The monk turned to Violet. "The blade must have been poisoned. They waited until he was out of the city to strike." The monk helped Robert lie down on his pillow.

Robert struggled to breathe. Violet broke free of the monk holding her shoulders and went to Robert's side.

"My quiver. Where is it?" he said between breaths.

"Where's the quiver?" Violet looked from one monk to the other.

The one by the door nodded toward the bed. Violet looked underneath it.

"He has no use for it now," said the second monk as he wiped Robert's brow.

Violet tossed him a burning look then put the quiver under Robert's blanket. "It's here, right beside you."

Relieved, Robert let his eyes close.

The monk shrugged impatiently. "A shopkeeper found it beside him."

His words ended abruptly when Robert grabbed the pail and was violently ill.

When he could speak, Robert said, "Violet." He searched about until his eyes settled on her. "You're safe."

Violet grasped his hand and sat beside him, confused. "Yes, I've been here all day, safe and sound."

Robert sighed and leaned his head back against the wall. "I was worried about you."

"About me?"

He grasped her hand weakly. "After they attacked me, I thought they might have done something to hurt you too."

The monk beside Violet said, "Nae doubt they were expecting you to collapse well past the city."

"I came back for Violet."

Violet shook her head. "I'm safe. Please don't worry about me."

Robert pulled her close enough to whisper into her ear, "Be on your guard, lass. You may not be safe here. As soon as I'm able, we're leaving. Be ready. Until then, you're no safer than I." With a cautious look, he released her to sit back up. He tried to get up but leaned back again.

Violet dabbed a cool, damp cloth on his forehead. "Rest now. We'll talk later."

His eyes closed.

One of the monks touched her shoulder and beckoned for her to follow him. In the corridor outside Robert's room, he spoke in hushed tones. "He must have kent he was poisoned and come back for help. He slid off his horse in a close outside a shop, where the shopkeeper found him and sent word to us."

Violet spoke softly. "Will he recover?"

"I dinnae ken. It is up to God now."

God was fine, but she wouldn't mind bringing in a modern doctor for a consult. But that couldn't be, so she went back inside and sat beside Robert while he slept. He was fitful. She blotted beads of sweat from his forehead. The monks went to supper and left her to tend to him, provided a monk remained with them for the sake of propriety, or so she assumed. After what Robert had said, she doubted the motives of everyone around them.

Violet Quinn was a practical woman. As an accountant, she did her best work with numbers and logical patterns. There was an inherent order to numbers that could always be relied upon. They could be managed and balanced until everything fell into place. She liked order in her life. That wasn't to say that she had no feelings, but she always felt best when her emotions were under control. But now she had lost all control. She found herself in a place where nothing made sense. Her journey through time had disrupted her sense of balance—both physical and emotional—and with what little remained, Sir Robert de Mallay had finished the job. He made everything else seem unimportant, which was why she needed more distance between them. She needed her head clear to think. But he was sick and in need of her help. He trusted her, and she wouldn't let him down.

To his credit, Robert had been quick to receive the message that they would be no more than travel companions. It was Violet who couldn't seem to live with her decision. Something inside her came to life in his presence. The sound of his voice drew her notice to the exclusion of others, and when he was in sight, every gesture, no matter how slight, enthralled her, for it was all part of him. She couldn't get enough of his presence, or touch, or the way that he listened and respected her wishes—such as when she asked him to leave her alone. Well, he hadn't done so well with that, but no one was perfect.

Violet whispered his name. She lifted his hand to her cheek. "Come back."

A soft sound came from his throat. She looked up. His eyelashes flickered then closed. Violet brushed the damp hair from his forehead then blew softly on his feverish brow.

They were never alone. She had tried to persuade the monks to go on with their usual duties, but the issue was nonnegotiable. Despite that, she wouldn't leave his side. So a monk sat in the chair, and she sat on the floor beside Robert's cot.

In the gray haze before dawn, she succumbed to her feelings. How could she deny that she cared? She had pushed him away because of her feelings for him, and it had worked. She had regained a sense of control over her emotions but at what cost? Would she miss out on a chance—perhaps her only one—to know love? No matter how short, this time could have been theirs. The thought brought tears to her eyes. She had wept when Jack had betrayed her, which was more than he had ever deserved. But this man deserved her tears and more. Her heart was so full of him that she could no longer hide from the truth. With a soft smile, she whispered his name.

"Don't leave me." She laid her head on the edge of his bed, and she wept.

A hand touched her head. Violet looked up to find Robert watching her. She clutched his hand and kissed it then rose to her knees and touched his forehead and face. Smiling through her tears, she looked at the monk then back at Robert, whose gaze rested on her.

"You've come back!" she said.

He tried to smile. "Are you weeping for me?"

"Don't flatter yourself." But she knew the relief in her eyes belied her words.

He brushed her cheek with his knuckles. She held his hand to her cheek, gazing into his eyes with unguarded affection. The corner of his mouth turned up a bit, then his eyes closed and he went back to sleep.

Monks came in and out through the day, checking on Robert as he slept, then speaking outside the room in hushed tones. At first Violet paid them no heed, caring little about their medical opinions—except to be ready to step in if they thought about doing something like bleeding him. But with increasing concern, she noticed their talk growing quieter, more urgent, and more secretive. Something was wrong, and whatever it was, they were not telling her.

When Robert woke next, one of the monks brushed past her and sat beside him. He spoke in tones too quiet for Violet to hear.

When he had left, Robert looked at Violet and forced a weak smile. "Would you fancy a walk?"

"You can barely sit up." The fact that he even suggested it made her question how lucid he was.

His eyes narrowed. "A walk in the courtyard would

do me good." He slung the quiver containing the scroll over his shoulder. It hadn't left his side since he had returned.

When he struggled to rise, Violet leaned down and whispered, "Have you lost your mind?" She took hold of his arm and helped pull him up.

Once standing, he smiled, leaned close, and spoke quietly. "We cannae talk here. Help me walk outside."

They passed two monks and walked through a stone arch to the courtyard. Violet helped ease him onto a stone bench.

"We must leave here tonight," he said.

Violet shook her head. "No, you're not strong enough yet."

He whispered, "But I will be alive—as will you. If we stay, neither of us will be for long."

Her eyes opened wide. Robert chuckled and cast a furtive glance toward a monk who was looking their way.

"Smile," Robert said. "Now lean over and whisper to me."

Violet did as she was asked. "You are scaring the crap out of me."

Robert laughed with what looked like genuine enjoyment, then he said softly, "I'm quite sure Henry knew the two men who attacked us and killed him."

"How do you know that?"

"After we arrived, two monks were sent to Perth to give Henry a proper burial. They found him where we'd left him, his throat cut ear-to-ear. But before they arrived, someone had gone back and cut off his hands and his feet."

"Why?"

"'Tis a Jesuit act against those who have betrayed them," Robert said.

"Henry?"

"Aye. He may have been planted to spy, or to find something they want."

Violet nodded. "Like the scroll."

"Exactly." Robert watched a monk walk through the cloisters from one arch to the next. "If he was a spy, he betrayed them when he fled with us."

"Then he betrayed you, as well."

"At some point, yes. Perhaps he had a change of heart, or he may have been spying on the Jesuits all along. All I ken now is that they've followed us here, and they're watching the monastery. No doubt they've got spies in here, as well."

A wave of dread passed through her, but she tamped it down and remained still. A telltale flush burned her cheeks as her heart pounded. "Why? I don't understand."

"I have the scroll. There must be something on it—or they believe that there is—that they dinnae want to be known. And since you've been with me, they'll assume that you've seen it as well."

Violet looked about the quiet courtyard, unable to reconcile the peaceful surroundings with what he was telling her. "They want to kill us? People here?"

"'Tis why I was attacked and why you're no more safe than I."

Violet looked at the monks all about, carrying on with their daily activities. "But here?"

He covered her trembling hand with his. "Do you trust me?"

She lifted her eyes, and his gentle look bolstered her courage. "Yes."

"I ken that you dinnae like to be told what to do." She inhaled, about to protest, but was interrupted when he said, "But if we're to survive, you must trust me and do as I say."

"Okay, but—"

"Without argument."

"Oh, c'mon!"

"We can argue all you like at the end of the day when we're safe."

She frowned.

With a crooked smile, he said, "I should warn you though, if we make it to the end of the day, then I will have been right. If not, you'll not have the chance to remind me."

"Well, that's just not fair." She nearly smiled, but it was a nervous and futile attempt. She steadied her gaze on him. "I don't have a choice. But if I did, I would still trust you with my life."

He tightened his hand about hers. "And I will protect it with mine."

CHAPTER 7
THE LEGACY

In the pre-dawn darkness, a drizzle sent darkening streaks down the stone walls of the Edinburgh buildings. Arriving at last on the cobbled streets, it left a damp sheen and the smell of wet stone. The uneven rolling of pushcarts was only beginning to awaken the city. From the bell tower, the abbot watched two robed figures slip through the friary gate and make their way through the long shadows, along narrow streets and even narrower wynds. At the same time, two more monks walked through a gate in the wall, and on the opposite side of the friary, a third pair of monks set forth on foot.

All of the monks were well on their way when dawn broke and a stable boy led a packhorse through the gate. He led his horse down the cobbled streets until he reached the edge of the city. From under a blanket, a man sat up and reached out his good arm to help the stable boy mount behind him. They rode south toward Roslin while, back in the city, three pairs of monks slipped back inside the friary gates.

After hours had passed, Robert and Violet pulled off the road to a place where water rushed down a hill and over some rocks. The horse needed water and rest, as did they. Robert helped Violet down then handed a bundle to her. Hiding behind a tree, Violet changed from her stable boy's clothes into her peasant bodice and skirts, while Robert pulled off his monk's robe. He tried to look strong and healthy, but he fooled only himself. He looked pale. She made sure that he ate some bannocks before they were on their way again.

For a long while, they rode in quiet, breathing the scent of fresh grasses. Morning sun barely shone through the faint veil of mist still clinging to the round wooded hills.

When Robert wearily exhaled, Violet said, "You're tired. You could use another day's rest."

"Whisht, woman. You worry too much."

"You must be feeling better, as grouchy as you are." She gave him a wry sideways look.

His only answer was an impatient grunt.

Violet suspected he was more fatigued than he would admit. If he wouldn't rest, she would try to distract him. "So how did you become a knight?"

"On a battlefield, after a battle."

"You must have done something brave to be honored like that."

"No more than any warrior would," he said.

"But there must be more to the story."

"No."

Violet nodded. So conversation wasn't going to happen. Silence settled once more between them.

By the time they stopped at midday, Violet could stand it no more. "What have I done?"

"Done?" Robert looked at her as though he doubted her sanity.

"Something's wrong. You won't talk to me. You're clearly frustrated or angry with me, and I don't even know what I've done."

He leaned forward and set his elbow on his knee. "What you've done?"

He looked genuinely angry, but Violet didn't regret having asked. At least now they could get it out in the open.

Robert looked away and heaved a deep sigh. "You've done nothing wrong."

Violet cast a sideways glance toward him. "Well, that just isn't true."

He shot her a piercing look while he spoke in a voice that was quiet and measured. "I would never lie to you."

Violet could neither think nor speak for a moment. When she did, it was all she could do to conceal the effect of his anger. She felt wounded, unsure, and a little bit angry. "I'm sorry. I just don't understand you."

"There's naught to understand." He walked away to the top of the brae and looked out at the glen.

The wind blew through the gentle green grass, which hissed as it yielded to form waves of silver. Violet watched him walk away. The smart thing would have been to let him go, let him keep his dark moods and thoughts to himself. She was better without them—or him. *And now who's lying?* She rose and went to him.

Without looking at her, he said, "I should have left

you in Perth." Violet took in a breath, preparing to argue, but he interrupted. "For your sake."

"Really?" Now it was Violet's turn to be annoyed. "You can't mean that."

"But I do."

"Have you forgotten that mob? I might have been trampled to death. Would you rather have left me to that?"

Robert nodded. "Possibly, but instead, you've been attacked—not once but twice—by what I believe are trained assassins. And now you are fleeing with a man whose good sense is clouded by his own foolishness."

Mouth agape, Violet tried to find the right words.

Before she could speak, he said, "'Tis time we left."

So that was that, according to Robert. Except that Violet was tired of him shutting her out. After what they had been through together, she didn't think asking for just a bit more disclosure was too demanding. For although he was honest, he withheld more than he shared. Perhaps that wasn't such a horrible trait, except when it left her in the dark, wondering what she had done or should do—or how he felt about her. Violet paused beside the horse before mounting.

She looked into his eyes. "Look, Robert, you've done everything right, and I'm grateful for it. I've never felt safer than when I'm with you."

He began to protest.

"No, now it's my turn to talk."

He stopped and gave her his rapt attention.

Violet inwardly smiled. "Thank you. Now, you've got to understand that you're not the only one making decisions around here. Everything that I've done, I have chosen to do. So stop acting as though you're the only one here making decisions—or making mistakes. We're in this together. Well, for now anyway."

They exchanged a look that was rich with emotions neither gave voice to. While she assumed she hadn't convinced him to stop beating himself up over how things had turned out, he looked almost appreciative. Well, at least he looked forgiven. So Violet mounted the horse and sank into Robert's arms as they rode away.

ABOVE THE TREE branches and leaves, pale gray washed the sky over Roslin. As they rode through the mottled shade of the woods, a dark-stoned Rosslyn Castle seemed to rise out of the solid cliff to form an imposing presence overlooking the trees rising out of a gorge. Robert and Violet rode over the bridge and into the bailey. The castle was a crumbling ruin with only portions of outer wall left. Robert took in the sight with a troubled brow.

Violet walked over to the only wall that remained of the keep and touched one of the vines twined into the stones. "How long has it been since anyone's lived here?"

Robert shook his head. "Not for a while, I imagine."

Violet looked about, shaking her head. "It would've been nice if someone had told us—to save us the trip."

"Aye, I was thinking the same. Well, I'll have a look about, then we'll inquire in the village as to where we might find William Sinclair." He walked over to a door that led to the most sound-looking portion of the remaining structure.

As he reached for the handle, a voice from behind him

spoke with an English accent. "He's away fighting border rebels."

Robert turned, expecting to see someone from the castle or village. Instead he found four men in black Jesuit cassocks, one holding Violet with his hand over her mouth.

One of them stood in front of the others. "Sir Robert. 'Tis a pleasure to see you again."

He had black hair and a scar under his left eye, and Robert recognized him as the priest he had pushed off the Brig of Earn. Robert looked straight into the priest's dark eyes. "Leave the lady out of this."

The priest smiled. "Oh, I wish that I could, but the lady is very much a part of it. But I will tell you this—if you give me the scroll, I'll not kill her."

"Nor harm her."

With a sly smile, the priest nodded. "Nor harm her."

Robert said, "I'll need more than your word."

"More than my word?" He assumed a wounded expression.

Robert eyed him with mistrust. "Swear to God, and by your Jesuit oath."

"My what?" the priest scoffed.

"You heard me. Swear that neither you nor your men will do harm to the lady."

With a light laugh, the priest said, "I swear before God and on my Jesuit oath that we'll not harm her."

Robert pulled off the quiver containing the scroll. "First let her go."

"Seize him," ordered the priest with a shrug. His companions forced the scroll from Robert's hands and started to drag him away, but the priest told them to stop.

"I don't want him to miss this. I've never been defeated until I met you. Now you'll pay for that privilege."

The priests led Violet and Robert to a hole in the ruined part of the castle.

"We're in luck. The oubliette is still here." The leader smiled at Robert. "Of course, 'tis not as refreshing as the River Earn, but it will have to do." He glanced at his men. "Put her in it."

The men tied a rope around Violet's waist and lowered her into the deep tubular hole. On the way down, she tried to climb back up hand over hand, but they dropped her suddenly, making her free fall the last few feet. One of the men warned her that if she didn't untie the rope and send it back up, they would pull her back up and make her wish that she had.

The leader smiled at Robert. "Oh, but we didn't give you a chance to bid your lady farewell."

Robert lunged at the priest, but two men held him back. All he could do was glare.

"Let him see her down there all alone—but unharmed —in the dark, lonely pit." The scar-faced priest gave him a crooked smile. "Now, I believe our business is complete." As he turned away and started to walk toward the village, he said, "Throw him over the edge."

Robert fought them, fueled not only by the drive to survive but for Violet, whose life depended solely upon his survival. They held no weapons, for they needed none. They struck with precision, almost too fast to be seen, let alone anticipated. Unlike any fighting he had seen, they used their hands as if they were spears or knives, then they jabbed with their elbows and knees. Robert had only his strength to oppose their uncanny speed and deft maneuvers, but he fought well. With his right fist, he landed a solid blow that sent one man staggering back. He followed with his left, while the others looked on as though entertained.

When he turned to them, one of them turned sideways and kicked while the other flipped him over to land on his back with a grunt. Tasting defeat, not to mention the dirt, he imagined Violet languishing in that oubliette until she died a slow, painful death, and a rage roiled within him that brought him renewed strength. He looked up to determine where each man was, then he sized up their strengths and chose the one he had the best chance of defeating. With a bellowing cry, he lunged for him.

But the others pulled him off their companion and used the momentum to back Robert to the edge of the stone wall that overlooked the ravine. He was bent backward over the ledge, his shoulders pressed hard by one priest while another grabbed his feet and upended him. By sheer force of will, Robert hung on and took the one holding him over the edge with him. The two fell, still struggling as they brushed past branches and twigs on their way down.

CHAPTER 8
NOT FORGOTTEN

The priest landed with his back wedged where the base of a branch met the thick trunk of a tree. With his fall partly broken by his now-dead attacker, Robert fell back from the branch as leaves rustled and twigs snapped. He randomly grasped for anything that might stop his descent until a branch caught his doublet and held him suspended. He struggled to breathe before the branch snapped, and he fell to a nearby branch below, where he held on. Secure for the time being, he thought of Violet and steeled himself for the climb down from the tree. Sharp pain shot through his chest to his side, but he forced himself to keep inching his way down the tree. From branch to branch, he proceeded with battered hands and unbearable pain in his ribs. A wrong move could send him to his death and Violet to hers, so by sheer force of will, he kept on, despite the blinding pain. He arrived at the last branch, which was ten feet from the ground. On another day, dropping to the ground would have been nothing, but he had not yet fully recovered from having been poisoned, and now he was sure he had cracked at least one rib. The drop to the ground would be his undoing. But he had to get Violet. So he fixed his mind on what had to be done, and he let himself fall.

He awoke, having passed out from the pain. How long he had been lying on the ground, he couldn't tell. Slowly, he rose and climbed up to the castle. He took a long way around to avoid the steep slope to the top. He was forced to stop to catch his breath, but breathing hurt more, so he trudged on. It was late afternoon by the time he arrived at the bridge to the castle.

He staggered to the opening of the oubliette. "Violet! Are you all right?"

A soft sob rose, followed by a long silence.

"Answer me, lass. Are you hurt?"

"No, I'm fine. I'm just glad to hear your voice!"

Robert looked about for the rope the others had used earlier. It lay cast aside by the crumbling castle wall. Robert bent to pick it up and cursed, holding his side. Not trusting himself to support her in his injured condition, he looked about for something to which he could secure the end of the rope. There was nothing near enough, so he looped the rope about his hips, well below his injured ribs, and dropped the other end down to her.

She tied it about her waist and called up, "Okay, I'm ready."

"Lass, can you climb at all?"

"A little. I climbed a rock-climbing wall on a cruise ship."

He puzzled over what that might mean but gave up. "Good. You climb, and I'll pull you up with the rope."

"Okay."

Robert leaned back, doing his best to use his weight to keep the rope taut. He had enough space behind him to keep backing up, rather than use his upper body to pull, which he could not have done. The mere act of breathing was painful enough. He would never have managed to pull her up on his own. From the length of the rope, she was nearly halfway to the top when the rope slipped and pulled against his cracked ribs. He would have cried out had he been able to take in enough air to do so. With his heels dug into the ground, he pulled back against the agonizing pressure. Unable to speak to even inquire about Violet, he focused on holding his ground.

Violet called, "Sorry! I slipped. I'm okay."

Robert was glad to hear that she was all right, even though he was not. Still, he kept pulling back until Violet's hand appeared over the top. Pulling on the rope hand over hand, he drew closer to her. All the while, he hoped neither of them would slip, for he didn't know whether he had the strength to keep her from falling. The top was flush with the ground, giving her nothing to grasp hold of, but Violet clutched at the edge while Robert dug in his heels and pushed back until she cleared the top. When he was sure she was safe, he lay back while pain coursed through his body.

Violet collapsed beside him and grasped his hand. "I thought I'd lost you."

He laced his fingers through hers and gave her hand a comforting squeeze while he winced. Breathing caused enough pain. He felt no need to talk.

Violet turned her head sideways. "You're hurt!"

"Aye."

Violet hovered over him. "Where? What can I do?"

He put his hand on her arm. "Calm yourself. I'll be fine."

"But you're not fine now."

His speech was labored. "'Tis my ribs. I may have broken one or two."

Violet smoothed back his hair from his forehead. "What can I do?"

Robert lifted his eyes to meet hers, and her gentle look moved him. Had he not been injured, he would have been tempted to pull her down and kiss her. But she had made it clear that she didn't want that from him, so his present state worked in her favor. Even so, he felt no compulsion to avert his gaze from the aquamarine eyes that searched his.

Her lips parted, and he thought she might kiss him after all. But instead—and to his disappointment—she spoke. "We should leave here. They could return."

Robert nodded but made no effort to move.

"How can I help you? Should I pull your wrists, or would it be better to push you up from your shoulders? Can you walk?"

Robert ignored her and pulled himself to a sitting position, where he stayed until the worst of the pain had subsided.

"We should bandage your ribs."

Without waiting for a reply, Violet tore her underskirt into wide strips and wrapped them around his chest. When she was finished, she helped pull him up to his feet, where he had no choice but to drape his arm over her shoulders and use her as a crutch. Well, at least there was one positive aspect.

She looked at him. "How did you ever manage to climb back up to the castle?"

He stared into her eyes without guile. "I had to. For you."

THE MAY SUN lingered into the evening, lighting their way as they set out for Perth. With their horse gone, no doubt taken by their Jesuit attackers, they walked over gently rolling hills, which were not so gentle when one was on foot and in pain. While she knew she fared better than he, she wasn't strong enough for the constant weight she was supporting. When they had been walking for an hour, she insisted that they stop to rest.

Robert was reluctant to speak, and Violet presumed that was because he was in pain. When they were far enough from the road to feel safe, she eased him down to sit against the trunk of an old gnarled oak, then she sat beside him, using the same trunk to support her. With a quiet moan, she rubbed her back, which had carried more than her share of the burden while walking.

"I'm sorry."

Too weary to lift her head from its resting place against the tree trunk, Violet said, "Sorry for what?"

"I should have listened to you and taken you to the cave when you wanted to go. You'd have been safe at home now."

With a shrug, she said, "Maybe."

Robert leaned his head back and closed his eyes.

A breeze troubled the leaves and stirred up scents of sweet vernal grass mixed with bluebells. Violet breathed in and smiled as she turned toward him. "But then I wouldn't have gotten to know what a hero you are."

With a smirk, Robert said, "Hero. There is no such thing."

"But there is—and you've been knighted. That proves it."

Robert narrowed his eyes. "Aye. And do you ken what that means?"

"You distinguished yourself in battle."

"Oh, aye. The lucky ones they call hero; they call all the other ones dead."

Violet could have said something encouraging, but he wouldn't have accepted it. She saw the dark mood on his face and knew there was nothing to say. The question was: how did she know that? She had known him for mere days, but in those few days, she had seen him—at his best and worst—and although she wouldn't tell him, she loved him. She wanted to believe that she loved who he was with no hope or expectation. That way it wouldn't hurt so much when they parted, which they would. Until then, they were friends—platonic ones. Plato would have been proud—if she hadn't been deluding herself.

He turned toward her, and her heart swelled. *Sorry, Plato.*

"I've let you down, Violet."

"That's crazy talk."

He shook his head. "And I've failed in the one task my parents left for me. I've lost the scroll."

Violet put her hand on his, but he snatched his away and turned from her. "God's blood, will you stop being so kind?"

She was taken aback. For a long while she stared at

him, thinking he would turn and apologize. When he did not, she looked the opposite way. She made an abrupt move to stand, and he flinched.

Violet suppressed the small measure of satisfaction she took in his pain. "Yes, I will." When he gave her a questioning look, she added, "I'll stop being kind." She extended her hand. "Now get up."

He looked at her, confused.

"You heard me."

"Aye, you're right. We should be on our way."

When he was standing before her, she looked him straight in the eyes—or as straight as she could, considering the fact that he had a good half dozen inches of height on her. "Get this straight: I went with you because it was my best option at the time. You're not responsible for me, so let go of that. And the scroll, well, I'm sorry, but it was a piece of linen. As much as your parents may have valued it, I'm sure that they valued you more. So stop beating yourself up now, and walk me to Perth."

Whatever emotions Robert was feeling, he kept to himself, except for the dark look in his eyes. Violet wished for words to ease Robert's self-loathing, but she knew of none. She knew only how deeply his feelings affected her. For that, there was a word, but she wouldn't voice it.

As they continued walking toward Perth, approaching hoof-beats sent them off the road and into the woods that lined this section of road. They had tried to avoid the road, but Robert was in so much pain that walking rough terrain was out of the question. So they walked the worn path, veering off when they heard others approaching. They waited for the rider to pass, but there no rider. The horse left the road and came straight to them. Robert started to laugh but was stopped by the pain. It was the horse they had ridden since Perth.

"There's a good lass!" Robert extended his palm and stroked its neck. Turning to Violet, he said, "Madam, your ride awaits you."

With that, they were on their way, bound for Perth. As they rode, Robert began to talk again, raising Violet's hope that his spirits were lifting, if only a little. When they were well away from Rosslyn Castle, they rode into a thickly wooded area and found a place Robert deemed safe for the night. In the last hours of light, he went looking for supper and returned with a wild hare.

When they had finished eating, Violet asked, "What will you do now?"

"What will I do?" He said it as if he were asking himself. "I'll take you home."

"And after that?"

He glanced at her then fixed his eyes on the embers left from the fire. "Since I can remember, I've had somewhere to live, an order to my days, and a future as a monk like the others around me. But I never really belonged. The scroll was a legacy from my parents. My father died for it. And now it's gone. What will I do now? I dinnae ken." Still in pain from his injuries, Robert struggled to stand. Violet rushed to his aid, but he grasped her wrist and held her at bay. "I can manage alone."

And he did. He managed alone for the rest of the night, but Violet did not. Late that night, she lay awake thinking of Robert, the man who had overcome overwhelmingly painful injuries to climb back up to the castle and save her from certain death. He had done that for her, but he wouldn't accept thanks. He would rather loathe himself for putting her in such a vulnerable position. But Violet didn't blame him. All she could think of was the sheer force of will that must have brought him back to save her. She could no longer deny that she was moved by his deep sense of devotion to whatever cause lay before him. But that was the problem. He had rescued her because it was the right thing to do, and in his absolute resolve to do the right thing, she'd caught a glimpse of his emotional strength, and her heart responded to it. More-over, it made her wonder what sort of devotion he might show to someone he loved, and she longed to find out.

CHAPTER 9
THE RETURN
TO PERTH

They arrived in Perth late the next evening, bypassing Edinburgh and, they hoped, their pursuers. Brother Thomas greeted them with warmth, which he extended to Violet as though the monastery were her home as well.

Seeing their reaction to the damage, Brother Thomas said, "The looters took everything they could find that had value and destroyed much that did not. But we're getting things back in order. Come, you must be hungry."

After they supped, Robert told Brother Thomas, "The scroll is gone."

Robert spoke simply, but Violet saw the dark look in his eyes. Brother Thomas listened while Robert explained, and Violet was struck by the quiet manner in which Thomas received news that must have been deeply upsetting.

Robert ran his fingers through his hair and leaned back in his chair with a deep, weary sigh that drew a wince that was not lost on Brother Thomas.

"What ails you, lad?"

"Och, 'tis only a bruise."

Violet flashed Robert a look then turned to Brother Thomas. "Or a break."

"Och." With barely a glance he dismissed her remark. "I still dinnae ken who they were, other than how they were dressed—in the cassocks of Jesuit priests."

Brother Thomas's brow creased.

"I've fought in battle and been knighted for my skill, but these men fought differently from any manner I've ever known. Not only were they fast, but they seemed to ken my next move, and they'd thwart it. I dinnae ken how I survived."

Brother Thomas nodded. "I think I ken who they could be. A small sect of Jesuits came back from Japan. They were missionaries there, and they learned a way of fighting that sounds like what you've described. I've no doubt they're after the Templars' secret knowledge."

Robert narrowed his eyes but said nothing.

Brother Thomas answered Robert's unspoken question, looking between him and Violet. "You know it already."

"Time travel?" Violet said it more to herself than to them.

Robert leaned closer. "And the scroll holds that secret?"

"I don't know. I was once told that it did, but I can't decipher the markings, except to guess that it might be some sort of map."

Violet asked, "Where would they take it?"

Brother Thomas met her question with a nod. "Where, indeed?"

"They may have already taken it to another time. If that's so, it will be nearly impossible to find now," Robert said with a frustrated frown.

Brother Thomas spoke in soft, even tones. "If they truly discover the secrets of time travel using the scroll as a guide, they could wreak havoc not only on our world but upon countless places and eras."

Robert leaned back and folded his arms over his chest then winced from the pressure against his ribs.

Brother Thomas leaned toward him. "What's the matter, lad?"

Robert shrugged. "Nothing."

Violet chimed in. "Nothing except that he's probably fractured a rib or two."

Robert looked away. "Och, 'tis just a few bruises."

Violet resisted the urge to argue.

Robert ignored their concern for his well-being. "They've got to be stopped."

"First, we must get the scroll back." Brother Thomas stared at the table with darkening eyes.

Robert absently ran his fingers along a line in the table as he thought.

Violet watched him, but her mind was elsewhere. "They could have hidden it anywhere by now. There's no way—unless..." Her eyes brightened as she and Robert shared a knowing look.

Robert leaned forward. "I must go back to a time before they took it."

Brother Thomas's silent stare was agreement enough.

VIOLET LAY AWAKE. After a long night with little sleep, morning came. As weary as she was, thoughts of the scroll, their attackers, and Robert weighed on her mind. Robert troubled her most, for she would soon have to leave him. That was why they'd returned to Perth. He would honor his promise to return her to the cave so she could go back to her world and the life she had known before. But that world wouldn't be the same for her now. Nothing would without Robert. But that was her problem, not his.

A quiet knock sounded at her cell door.

"I'm taking you back to the cave." Robert averted his eyes. "We must leave now if we're to reach it before dawn. We're more likely to journey through time when the cave gets the most sunlight."

She wasn't sure what she had expected him to say, but that made her heart sink. With as much cheer in her voice as she could muster, she said, "Okay." She slipped on her shoes and stood, ready to go.

The sky glowed a dim gray through the mist as they made their way to Kinnoull Hill. All was quiet, except for Violet's skirts brushing against the tall grass. From time to time, Robert cautioned her to watch her step, but otherwise, they were silent. By the time they reached the foot of the hill, Violet had imagined a dozen things she might say when they parted, none of which she would ever give voice to. When she dared let her eyes meet Robert's, she saw the same troubled spirit. He, too, kept his words in check, for they both knew it was better that way. Instead, Violet kept her mind on the climb. She knew the path a bit better now, which helped. But the height had not changed, nor had her bothersome skirts. Still, they managed to reach the cave before dawn. Once inside, they stood facing each other.

When her eyes met his, her resolve faltered. "Thank you." The words sounded formal, as if she'd said them at the close of a business meeting.

Dark eyes met hers. "Aye, well, you're welcome." He lifted her hand and stared at it as though he might say more, but he didn't. He just stared at her with a determined expression.

The sun burned through the thinning mist to the back of the cave. Violet whispered, "I have to go."

Robert nodded, his jaw set.

She turned and walked away. Their hands touched until the last step took her beyond his reach, then she turned and stood, waiting. The sun shone brilliantly into the cave as she took her last sight of Robert through tears. She felt a surge of power as though she were leaving, and a sob escaped. Then dark clouds blew in and darkened the sky, and the sensation of leaving was gone. Tears trailed down her cheeks as Robert pulled her into his arms. She clung to him and wept. Robert wiped tears from her face and kissed her.

"I don't understand what just happened." Violet buried her face in his neck and breathed in his scent. "But I'm glad." She looked up, and his gray eyes softened.

"Are you?"

"Can't you tell? You're soaked through from my tears." She smiled and smoothed her fingertips over his damp shoulder.

His intense gaze bore through her. "Why?"

Violet looked down to avoid his eyes.

"Say it," he insisted.

"Why?" She looked up and shook her head. "What's the use?"

"Because since I've met you, you've pushed me away."

Violet took in a breath to protest, but he lifted an eyebrow, which stopped her. Of course he was right. But what good was it to pretend they could have any sort of a future—or even a present? She was on her way home.

He held her shoulders and made it nearly impossible for her to look anywhere but at him. "I'll not force myself on you. Nor will I take advantage of your somewhat over-wrought state." He practically smiled.

She fought an urge to smile back.

He smoothed her hair back from her face. "All I ask is the truth."

Calmed by his voice and his presence, she glanced outside but barely noticed the clouds rolling by, making way for the sun. She was with Robert, which was more important than anything else. For no matter what happened, she wanted to tell him the truth, so that he would know and remember. "I love you."

That was all Robert needed to draw her into a kiss—and another. Untroubled by the tears spilling freely from her eyes, he was practically laughing. "I think I've loved you since I saw you hugging that cliff face."

She grinned while wiping her tears, but her smile faded. "And then you were there, and you've been there when I wasn't sure where or how to go on."

"With me."

"What?" She did not dare trust herself to believe what he had said.

Before he could answer, they looked outside. The clouds had all gone. Sunlight poured into the cave.

Violet looked at Robert. "Something's happening."

"Aye." While the world changed before them, they clung to one another. Power surged through them, and the world went black.

ROBERT EXHALED in relief as Violet opened her eyes. She met his concerned look with apparent confusion, then she tried to sit up.

He swept his arm underneath her and helped her. "Are you all right?"

"Yes, I think so."

They stepped out of an ancient stone structure and into a field with no one else in sight. Colored leaves seemed to murmur in the trees as a breeze made her shiver. A short distance away was an octagonal stone chapel.

"What is this place?" she asked.

Robert's eyes fixed on the chapel. "I've heard it described. If I'm not mistaken, it's Laon. We're in France."

"I don't understand. I was going home. You were with me."

Robert felt as disconcerted as she looked. "It's a Templar chapel. I was going to come here after you went home. My parents were here when King Philip's men arrested the Templars."

When Violet opened her mouth to ask a question, soldiers appeared on the horizon.

Robert gripped her arm. "God's wounds! It's happening now. We must go to the chapel!"

They ran and ducked inside the chapel, where a Templar spoke in hushed tones to a nun.

Wasting no time with formalities, Robert said in French, "The king's men are coming. We must—"

The Templar and nun turned, alarmed. Robert froze, his eyes fixed on the Templar.

Violet took in a sharp breath then whispered, "Brother Thomas!"

The Templar looked strangely at her and answered in English. "Do I know you?"

She nearly said yes, but the truth was that it would be years before he would know her. How many? Her accountant's mind started to calculate. The time between now and the sixteenth century would be two hundred fifty-two years. But not counting the years that they time traveled past, what was left? Robert had not been born yet but would be in less than a year, so that meant that another twenty-five years would pass before she would meet Thomas. Her head hurt.

Before Violet could reply, Robert appeared to regain his composure. "Sir Thomas?"

"Yes."

"You speak English?"

"I do. What troubles you?"

Robert visibly shook off his shock at finding Thomas there and focused on the immediate threat. "The king's men are riding this way. They're rounding up Templars. If they find you here, they'll arrest you—or worse." Robert looked sharply about. "Is anyone else here?"

Thomas shot a dark look at Robert. "No. Come with me." Grasping the nun's elbow, he led the way to a heavy oak door that led to a small room.

Violet whispered to Robert, "But if no one else is here, then he must be—"

"Aye." Robert tightened his hand about hers and gave her a pointed look that made clear his desire for her to be silent. It was clear to him as well that the people before him were his parents. The man he had known all of his life as Brother Thomas was his father. How could he not have told him?

"Mademoiselle, you must hurry." Thomas sent Violet and the nun through a heavy oak door that led to a small side room, then he turned to urge Robert to enter.

"One moment." Robert went to the altar. "Where is it? Where's the scroll?"

Thomas hesitated and glanced toward the altar.

"Hurry! Get the scroll. You cannae leave it behind!" Robert cast a nervous look toward the outside door, where the king's men would soon enter.

Thomas scrutinized Robert for a moment, then he went back to retrieve the scroll from under the altar. They rushed into the side room, where Thomas sprang a hidden latch. A panel swung open to reveal a tunnel. One after the other, the four people climbed into the narrow passageway and proceeded along its dark path. The latch closed with a click just as the king's men burst into the room off the chapel. Having made their escape, the four followed the tunnel to its end, where a ladder led up to a hatch that opened in the midst of a thick copse of trees surrounded by farmland. Inside the tunnel, they hid, waiting in silence for darkness to fall, alert to any sound that might signal the soldiers' approach.

No one dared even whisper. In that stillness, Robert suffered. His one saving grace was feeling Violet's arm slip through the small space left by his bent elbow. She rested her head on his shoulder and put her other hand over his. They couldn't talk, but he knew that she understood how his life and his place in the world had been shaken by Thomas's actions. There was no longer anything he could count on, except that his life had been built upon a lie. Even if he could talk to his father, what would he say? In the present year, he had not yet been born. Neither parent knew him or what was to come. If he told them who he was, what help would it be? He couldn't confront them and ask them to justify choices they had not yet made. Telling them what to do would, at best, confuse them and, at worst, further alter the path his life would take. He had no way of knowing what the ramifications would be. The better course was to wait until he was back in his own time to confront Brother Thomas, or rather Sir Thomas, as he would have to address his father for now since he was a Knight Templar. That assumed he would make it back to that time. For now, he didn't know whether he had a future beyond the next few minutes or hours.

Violet slid her fingers along his palm and twined her fingers in his. He wasn't facing this alone, and that brought him comfort.

CHAPTER 10
THE DOLMEN

The king's men left sometime in the hours before dawn. The four travelers emerged from the tunnel and looked about. Robert briefly but clearly explained that he and Violet had come through the dolmen from some distance hence. When Thomas and his mother accepted that without question, he knew they were aware of its power. So the four of them made their way there. The moon hung low in the sky and, with the faint glow of dawn, lit their path through the trees.

They were faint shadows making their way, which was better for Robert. As close to the surface as his feelings were, it was better that his companions not see him, lest he betray how he felt. He needed more time to find his way through the tangle of emotions before he could manage to look his father in the eye. It wasn't in Robert's nature to sidestep the truth. After all, he was a warrior trained to confront whatever got in his way. He faced his fear and ran straight toward danger to fight for what was right. Now he couldn't even confront his father to ask him why he had raised him with the lie that his father was dead. What sort of man let a young child believe that? But the man before him had done nothing wrong yet. And the woman before him was his mother. Months from now, she would die giving birth to him. He wanted to thank her for all she had done—and would do—for him. But how could he do so without telling her that the man before her was her unborn child fully grown? No, it was best to say nothing.

They arrived at the dolmen as sunlight brushed the horizon. Violet slipped her hand into Robert's and strengthened him. For the true strength of a warrior lay in his heart, and now Violet was there. The sun was fully upon them. The couples held hands as they lifted their faces to its bright warmth.

Robert extended his hand. "Sister—?"

"Sister Claudine," she said with a faint smile as she grasped Robert's hand.

And then they were gone.

ROBERT RECOVERED FIRST and sat up, relieved to see the familiar stone walls of the Dragon Hole. Thomas stirred, and the women soon after. Sister Claudine tucked in wisps of hair that had escaped from her wimple. Her hair was straight and black, like Robert's. They slowly made their way down to the foot of the hill, where they rested before embarking on foot for Perth.

Once safely on the ground, Robert discreetly studied his parents. Sir Thomas was much the same, but he had the exuberance of one who had not yet suffered loss. Sister

Claudine kept a proper distance from Sir Thomas, barely looking at him. Only once did Robert catch a fleeting glance between them, and that single glance was evidence enough of their love. The look in her eyes was enough for Robert to understand why Sir Thomas would break any vow to be with her. Her gentle brown eyes suggested inner warmth that would be hard to resist. Robert found comfort in seeing the love his parents shared, but the comfort was tinged with the sorrow of knowing their fate.

Robert stole glances at Violet whenever he thought he might falter. His sense of who he was had always been his foundation. As little more than a foundling, he had constructed a sense of his worth based on sheer will and a vision of who he wanted to be. And he had achieved it. He was a strong and honorable knight who not only believed in what was right, but he acted upon it with all of his might. When he'd found out that Brother Thomas was really his father, he felt angry, betrayed, but most deeply hurt. But Violet was there. For how long, he couldn't be certain, so he chose to save that question for another time.

An hour later, they arrived at the Blackfriars Monastery, where Robert was relieved to discover that there was not a second Brother Thomas already there, but there was a young abbot, who would have been in Perth just before Robert was born. So they seemed to have arrived at least near the time they were supposed to. Father Abbot arranged for them to be fed then came the questions. Robert did his best to hide his surprise as Sir Thomas launched into a tale of how he and Sister Claudine had left their monastery in France to seek a different way to serve God. Thomas claimed they had come over by ship from Calais to Leith, where they had met up with

Robert and Violet—who were married, according to Sir
Thomas. For safety, as well as propriety, they thought it
best not to travel alone, so they all came together.

"Is that not so, Sir Robert?" Sir Thomas met Robert's
eyes with a composure that Robert admired.

A few seconds too late, he replied, "Yes." His nod was
a bit too pronounced, but it was the best Robert could do
when presented with so thoroughly false an accounting of
their journey together.

Thomas continued. "Our travel companions must
regrettably leave in the morning to continue their
journey."

"Oh, and where to?" Father Abbot looked straight at
Robert.

"Inverness."

And that, along with some cordial conversation, was
the extent of Robert's part in the lie. During their walk to
Perth, Robert had cautioned Violet not to speak around
others, lest she reveal her strange accent and prompt more
questions than they had answers for.

Father Abbot turned his attention to Sir Thomas and
Sister Claudine. "Of course I will have to seek permission
with the bishop for your transfer, Sister. As you know,
you cannot simply move about as you please. There is a
process, and it can take time. In the meanwhile, you are
welcome to stay here." His eyes drifted to Sister Claudine,
whose cheeks were stained with a blush.

Robert suspected the color in her cheeks came from
fear. He imagined she wasn't used to lying. With a quick
glance, Robert checked to see if the abbot might wonder
the same, but the young abbot regarded her with an alto-
gether different look in his eyes. It was one of appraisal,

which made Robert uneasy. But a quick glance at Sir Thomas showed no similar suspicion on his face, so Robert decided he had misread the abbot, and he set aside his concern. So matters were settled with relative ease. His parents would settle into life at the Blackfriars Monastery, and Robert and Violet would leave in the morning.

Sir Thomas leaned forward. "There was one additional matter remaining."

Robert shot a pointed look at his father. "Sir Thomas, the hour grows late. Any other matters in need of discussion can surely wait until tomorrow."

Sir Thomas returned Robert's glance with narrowing eyes then gave him a nod. "Yes, of course." Turning to the abbot, he said, "It's been a long and tiring day for all of us." His eyes swept over the women then returned to the abbot. "May we please have your leave to retire for the evening?"

"You may. We shall find time to speak in the morning."

They all rose and bade farewell to the abbot before proceeding down the hallway to their rooms for the night. The women were first to be escorted to their cells. When Sister Claudine turned to bid them all good night, her eyes settled on Robert. His throat tightened, but he managed a cordial good night. She lifted her eyes to his and smiled. He hoped to always remember that smile and the kindness in her eyes.

Robert closed the door to his cell and lay down on the narrow cot. He would wait to go see Sir Thomas until he was sure everyone was asleep. Until then, he would think of a way to get the scroll from the young Thomas—even if he had to steal it. Otherwise, he would have failed in the mission his father had entrusted to him, and he wouldn't do that.

It was still dark when Robert tapped on Sir Thomas's door. Once inside, he told the truth about what had happened to the scroll. After all, Thomas had already experienced time travel, so convincing him that Robert came from the future wouldn't be an impossible task. The greater challenge would be convincing Sir Thomas to let Robert take the scroll for safekeeping. Having only just met, Thomas could think that Robert had any number of plans for the scroll, none of which the young Sir Thomas would approve.

Robert had one final truth to explain, so he said it simply. "I am your son."

Emotions flashed through Sir Thomas's eyes until the possibility of its truth at last settled on him.

"Sister Claudine is my mother." The truth of her death weighed on Robert as he looked at his father. He would never tell Thomas that piece of the future, for there would be agony enough when it happened. "I was raised as a foundling. No one ever knew your secret." When Thomas remained silent, Robert realized the rest of the truth. "You didnae ken."

"She's with child?" Thomas turned away. When he had regained his composure, he wiped his face and turned back to Robert.

From the way Thomas peered at him, Robert wondered whether his father was examining each feature and ascribing it to one parent or the other. Perhaps that convinced him more than any words Robert could say, for Sir Thomas spoke as if saying the words might make sense of it. "Robert. My son."

Sir Thomas gestured toward a chair. Robert sat while Thomas sat on the edge of his cot.

"I was young and full of dreams and ideals when I joined the Templars," Sir Thomas said. "I could see only the glory of doing God's work. And there was glory, but there also was hardship and blood. It wore down my ideals until I wanted nothing more than to go to the country and live the life of a peasant, doing simple things. That is what I eventually did. I returned to France and, as I worked, found the peace I had lost."

Sir Thomas's eyes lit with a fond smile. "I met Sister Claudine when she was quite newly arrived. They sent her to farm in the fields, but she was too gentle-born to know what to do. They lost patience with her, so they assigned her to me. At that time, I oversaw the relics and copied texts. My days, between prayers, were filled with the preparation of inks, preparing parchment, and copying texts into illuminated books. Claudine was a gifted student and an engaging friend to talk to.

"She was the ward of an uncle who had chosen her life for her, according to cost. Since being a nun was cheaper than getting married, she found herself there. As full of life as she was, she had never been given the chance to live. It was different for me. I had made my own choice, and I had been in the world and seen what it could be. By then, I was content to live my life apart.

"Claudine was everything good about life and the world. I looked forward to each day beside her. I knew my feelings for her had grown beyond what was proper, but I convinced myself that as long as I never expressed them, my feelings would do no one harm. But one day we were bent over a book we were working on, and our hands were so close. She told me she was taking her vows on the morrow. I traced a blue vein along her hand, and my resolve shattered. I poured out my heart, and she told me she loved me. We met in secret that night, and we lay in each other's arms and dreamed of a future together. But what future was there for us? She was riddled with guilt, for although she had taken no vows yet, she blamed herself for causing me to break mine. We wanted to run away, but where to? I had no means to support her. We talked in circles until dawn then hurried back to our cells before anyone missed us. That afternoon, I watched her say her vows, knowing that she loved me." Thomas choked back bitterness. "Later she told me that she would not have me stumble alone. Whatever happened, we would be together."

Robert gripped his father's shoulder then sank onto a wooden chair and buried his face in his hands. He was with a man near his own age, who loved as he loved. But the man was his father. Sir Thomas put a hand on Robert's shoulder. Using sheer strength of will, Robert calmed himself and looked up.

"If you dare trust me, I swear I will take the scroll somewhere safe." Robert held up his palm. "But before you trust me, I must tell you about it." Robert explained what had befallen the scroll.

When he was through, Sir Thomas retrieved the scroll from under the bed. "Guard it well, my son. See that it is put safely back in the hands of the Templars."

"I will." Robert took the scroll, and the two men embraced.

"You're a fine man. I'll credit your mother with that." Sir Thomas smiled.

Robert smiled back, but grief caught in his throat, for he knew that his mother wouldn't have the chance to shape his character. That task would fall to his father.

Just as he was about to leave, Robert turned back. "Tell me something. I need to get back to 1559, but the last time we went to the cave, instead of taking us where we wanted to go, it brought us here."

His father gave the question some thought. "From my travels and those of the Templars I've known, I can only surmise that where travel through time is concerned, we are ruled by our destiny. Some might call it God's will, yet I have seen men make choices that fly in the face of anything God could possibly want them to do. Perhaps the power is found in the stones themselves. I only know that there are no mistakes. We are taken where we need to be, even if we do not always understand."

Robert's brow creased. "I was meant to meet you like this?"

Sir Thomas smiled. "I would like to think so, but perhaps it has more to do with Claudine or Violet—perhaps even the scroll. If it is meant to be somewhere, then it's possible no one can truly destroy it."

Robert nodded. "I would like to think that."

Sir Thomas said, "You are not God. You are merely a man. If you fail in your mission, someone else will succeed."

"But I want to succeed."

"Of course you do. But if you worry about things you

cannot control, you'll be of less use to anyone. Give your all, then do not look back." With that, he embraced Robert. "Godspeed, my son."

Robert left with the scroll and a dozen questions his father wouldn't be able to answer until he was older. So he went down the hall to Violet's cell and tapped on her door. The door opened, and Violet slipped silently into the hall.

CHAPTER 11
THE SEA VOYAGE

A ship bound for Orkney sailed from Perth Harbour at dawn with Robert and Violet upon it. After stops at two ports on the way, their ship pulled into Wick Harbour, where Robert and Violet disembarked. She clung to Robert's arm, feeling weak from the seasickness she had suffered the full length of the journey.

As they walked along the busy quay, Robert said, "Will you not even try to ride?"

Violet shook her head. "Right now, it's all I can do to walk. And you know how I feel about riding. I have tried. It didn't go well. Can't you forgive this one flaw? It's my only one." She lifted her eyes, fully expecting him to laugh.

Robert suppressed a smile. "I suppose that I can."

Violet slipped her hand around his elbow. "You're too good to me, Robert."

"Aye." He grinned and kept walking until they found a stable with horses for hire.

Minutes later, they were riding along the coastline from Wick to Castle Girnigoe. Violet lifted her face to the wind and took in the staggering beauty. Steep, rough-sided cliffs faced the edge of the water with a defiance that dared the sea to confront them, which it did with unforgiving persistence. The wildness of this place appealed to her, and she found herself longing to stay.

Before long, the castle came into view. Jutting out into the water, it looked as bold as the rough cliff that formed its foundation. They presented a letter from Brother Thomas, which gained them admission to the castle and inside the keep. They were led to some chairs beside an inviting fire, where they waited. Soon a male servant entered and asked them to come with him. They were led into a library, where a gentleman sat at a desk. After introductions, John Sinclair, 3rd Earl of Caithness inquired about their journey and spoke of the weather, by which time, all were comfortably seated. By now, Violet was used to being introduced as Robert's wife. He had convinced her that doing so made their traveling alone together more proper.

Robert said, "My Lord, I've come to deliver something that was entrusted to me with instructions to leave it in the hands of a Sinclair."

Lord Caithness lifted a brow, clearly intrigued. Robert offered him the quiver containing the scroll. He took it with interest and removed the scroll. As he uncoiled the linen, his eyes widened.

With a quick glance at Robert, he said, "Do you ken what this is?"

"Not entirely, no. Two hundred years ago, a Templar knight left it with the Blackfriars for safekeeping. Circumstances are such that we now feel it should be in the hands of a Sinclair. It is now where it belongs." Robert maintained his posture, but his shoulders relaxed now that he was eased of his burden.

Lord Caithness eyed Robert quizzically. "Do you ken what it says?"

Robert shook his head. "My lord, I am only the messenger. But I do ken its value and that some would have it for themselves. It would be best to find a safe place to hide it."

Lord Caithness gave a somber nod. The next moment, his mood shifted. He smiled first at Violet then Robert. "Will you stay and sup with us?"

With a quick glance at Violet, Robert turned to his host. "Thank you for your generous offer, my lord, but I'm afraid we must be on our way. We're for Perth in the morning."

With a nod, Lord Caithness thanked Robert for his service in delivering the scroll and wished them both well.

With the scroll safely ensconced in Castle Girnigoe, they left the castle and rode alongside the cliffs on their way back to Wick.

Robert had been quiet since leaving the castle, so Violet glanced back and said, "You must be relieved."

"I've done what I set out to do."

"Yes, you have. And that must bring a good feeling."

He answered with a grunt.

BY THE TIME their ship pulled into Perth Harbour, Violet had made up her mind not to board a ship ever

again. The North Sea had afflicted her with the worst
seasickness she had ever known. Soon after their feet
touched ground, Robert found them a room in an inn,
where she could rest and regain strength enough to climb
the hill to the cave so they could travel back to the Perth of
Robert's time. Although he was reluctant to admit it, he
was not fully recovered from his injuries, so he welcomed
the rest.

Every part of her trembled as Violet attempted to
climb the stairs in the inn. Robert slid his sturdy arm
about her waist and practically lifted her, step by step, to
the top of the stairs. Part of her fought her dependence
upon him, but as weak as she was, that part lost. Unable
to manage on her own, she was grateful for his strength
and was reassured by his confidence. He had reason to be,
for he was a formidable man. But for all of the power he
wielded with a sword, his tenderness astonished her most.

As if reading her thoughts, Robert pulled back the
covers and set her gently upon the bed. As he tucked the
bed linens about her, he said, "I'm afraid it's not so nice a
room as you're used to in your time, but 'tis the nicest I
could find."

Violet lay with her eyes shut and sighed. "It's not a
swaying hammock on a ship's gun deck, which makes it
heaven." She tried to smile but gave up.

The corner of Robert's mouth turned up as he bent
to place a soft kiss on her forehead.

SUN SHONE through leaded panes as Violet awoke with
terrible thirst but without the nausea that had plagued her

since boarding the ship. A night's sleep on dry land had cured her. She rolled over to get up and find water, but an arm repositioned itself over her. Robert had fallen asleep by her side. He had been with her every night of their travels but never in her bed. On the ship, although he had rarely left her side, they each slept in a hammock. To feel him spooned against her felt good and right. She belonged in his arms.

"Are you all right?" His breath was warm on her neck.

Violet smiled. "I'm thirsty. I was going to get some water."

He placed a soft kiss just behind her ear then got up, went to the pitcher and basin, and poured a cup of water. He sat on the bed beside her while she drank it. Violet finished and set the cup on a bedside table. Robert absently followed her hand with troubled eyes.

Before she could ask what was on his mind, Robert said, "Are you able to eat?"

"Yes, I'm much better."

With a nod, he said, "Good. Then we'll break our fast then go to the cave. We'll try to go home—to my home, that is—if you're up to it."

"Yes, I'll be fine. Robert, is something the matter?" Violet searched his dark eyes.

His face brightened as he shook off his mood. "Oh, aye. I've a fierce hunger." He put his hand over hers. "I'll go see about having some breakfast brought up."

"No, I'll go with you." Robert started to rise, but Violet gripped his sleeve and pulled him back down. "Don't go."

She leaned closer and managed a kiss before he gently

but surely put his hands on her shoulders and put distance between them. After all they had been through—and after confessing their love—they were in a room with a bed, and she wanted more than his words. She wanted him. But instead, he arose and got dressed.

Violet hugged her knees to her chest. "Robert?"

Without looking up, he pulled on his boots. "Aye?" When she did not answer, he looked at her.

She studied him for a moment. "What's on your mind?"

His questioning look dissolved as a grin took its place. "Food!" He gave her a kiss on the forehead then went to the door, where he paused. "Take your time, lass. I'm away to make sure that a fine feast awaits you when you come downstairs."

He was gone before she could respond.

For the rest of the day, Robert was attentive but distant. The odd mixture confused her, but he evaded any attempt at serious conversation. After her first few attempts—which he fielded with a skill she could not help but find impressive but also transparent—she gave up and accepted his light, playful mood. It was a new side of him she hadn't seen. Since she had met him, they had always been under pressure, and often in danger, as they sought to deliver the scroll. With that accomplished, the burden was lifted. Perhaps that was all that this mood of Robert's was: his desire not to worry—or even to think. Was he not entitled to that much?

So Violet and Robert enjoyed their day, slowly working toward the cave. Their plan was to arrive at the cave before dark and to spend the night there. Robert insisted that Violet stop to rest often. She needed to save strength for the climb, which went well.

Violet would have liked to think that her climbing skills had improved, but in fact, having Robert close behind her, coaching with his strong arms at the ready, had more to do with it. Although having him so close was its own distraction, she wasn't complaining. As preoccupied as Robert had been throughout the day, she took what closeness she could get with a measure of gratitude, though she was still somewhat frustrated. Robert's mood grew worse.

By the time their only light came from the fire Robert had lit at the mouth of the cave, Violet said, "I can't take any more. You've got to tell me."

"Tell you what?"

Violet took a deep breath and exhaled. "What I've done. You've been brooding all day. For the past hour, I've carried on a one-woman conversation, and—fascinating as I might be—I could use some input."

"Some what?"

"Input. Oh, sorry. It's a computer term."

"Computer?"

"Never mind. My point is: are you angry with me?"

Robert's eyes widened. "Angry? With you?"

Violet met his shocked look with a frank look of her own. "It can happen—and has, more than once."

"Not with me. Well, perhaps once—when you ran away to the bridge." He stared off into the distance for a moment. "Then there was the fact that you wouldnae even try to learn how to ride. Oh, and—"

"Never mind!" Violet held up her hands to stop him.

"Point taken. But let's just talk about today. You've been in a very dark mood."

"Aye, I suppose I have."

"There's no supposing about it. You have, and I want to know why."

Robert moved closer to Violet and put his arms about her. He held her face and kissed her. "I'm sorry." He kissed her again.

Putting her brain on hold, Violet let him kiss her. His ploy nearly worked, for her priorities practically shifted. It was he who inadvertently set her back on course. As they kissed and she sought to be closer to him, he backed away in what had become a recent pattern—a pattern she did not enjoy. That reminded her of her original question: his mood—his foul mood, truth be told—which he had repeatedly refused to explain.

"'I'm sorry' isn't an answer," she said.

"I'm afraid I've nothing better to offer. 'Tis my own problem, and I'll work it out."

"Can't you talk about it?"

"Talking doesnae make everything better."

Violet let out a frustrated sigh as she stared at the fire. "Fine."

Robert squeezed her shoulder and kissed her forehead. "I'm glad you understand."

Violet turned to unleash her annoyance upon him. "Oh, I never said that I understood. I'm just accepting defeat."

He took her chin gently and leaned closer. "It's not a battle."

"Isn't it?" Violet tried to be strong, but she couldn't hide her worries. It didn't help that he deliberately closed the distance between them until his mouth was inches from hers, especially when the memory of his last kiss was still on her lips.

He gazed into her eyes. "No, it has nothing to do with us."

"Are you sure?" As soon as she said it, she regretted how needy she sounded. He had answered her question— not well, but it was the best she would pry out of him. She switched to a more logical approach and spoke gently. "Never mind. I was worried, but I get it. You don't want to talk. We don't have to. I understand."

That went well, except for the part that she spoke with false words. She didn't understand, and she wanted to talk. Violet was beginning to understand why she had bad luck with men. Luck had so little to do with it.

But to her surprise, Robert took her words at face value and went one better. "There's a good lass."

Violet winced. Oh, well, it wasn't a great start, but his finish was strong. He slid his hand to the nape of her neck and kissed her with a candor his words clearly lacked. Apparently in lieu of actual words, kisses and touches were quantifiable benchmarks of love. Still, she had questions—and a hand that was now at the small of her back and still moving. *Oh, screw metrics.* She was on board with this new standard of measurement.

He abruptly got up and leaned on the cave wall, staring outside.

"Robert?"

Without turning around, he said, "I'll not have a child of mine grow up a bastard."

Violet didn't know how to respond.

He turned toward her and paced a few times. "We

dinnae ken where we will be in a week, let alone for the rest of our lives. Until we do, I'll not risk putting a child through what I went through." He sank down and sat against the wall.

All she could manage was a nod, for his sorrow made her heart ache.

CHAPTER 12

THE FRIARY

T he journey back to Robert's sixteenth century time went as well as Violet's fear of heights would allow. As she and Robert walked through the gateway into the Blackfriars Monastery, Violet felt at ease. "It's a little like coming home. Of course, for you, it is home."

"Aye."

Given his gruff tone, his answer was mercifully short. Coming home had done nothing for his spirits. Violet did her best to ignore it, as she had all day.

Before long, his father approached them. Robert was not only aloof to Brother Thomas; he was barely polite. His manner didn't escape Brother Thomas's notice, but he deflected any awkwardness by inviting them to join the others at supper, which had just begun. As soon as his father looked away, Violet gave Robert a sharp look and was met with a clenched jaw as he turned away.

So that was what Robert had been agonizing over. She should have known better than to believe he had handled it well when he first learned the truth. He had said nothing about it to her or to young Brother Thomas. Why would he have? The young Brother Thomas didn't know who Robert was, nor had he yet lied to him. Robert had no quarrel with him—not yet. Violet realized that Robert had been biding his time, saying nothing to anyone until he and his father were alone.

Violet was grateful to Brother Thomas and the monks at their table for the supper conversation, since Robert's monosyllabic responses made it clear he did not wish to talk.

When supper was over, they began to head back to their cells, but Robert stopped Brother Thomas. "May I have a word?"

Brother Thomas may not have noticed, but Violet heard the edge in his voice.

Brother Thomas pleasantly nodded. "Yes, but I'm sure you're exhausted. We can talk in the morning."

"We can talk now." There was no mistaking the edge in Robert's voice.

His father eyed him warily. "All right. Let's go to my workshop."

"Good. I'll escort Violet to her room, and I'll meet you there." Robert started to lead her by the elbow.

"No." She looked from one surprised face to the other. "You're not going to shuffle me off so you can have man talk."

In a quiet voice, Robert said, "This isnae the time for this."

Violet lifted her chin and met Robert's eyes. She said softly, "It is, and I'm going with you."

It was no victory when he surrendered. He was

choosing his battles and timing. Violet knew well that her battle was still coming. They walked along the cloister to the workshop.

Once inside with the door closed, Robert wasted no time. "I should have kent what a liar you were when I saw you making false relics for donors."

Brother Thomas's eyes closed for a moment, then he looked straight at Robert.

When he offered no argument, Robert went on. "I grew up thinking my father was dead."

Brother Thomas nodded. "I regret that."

Eyes blazing, Robert said, "Do you? Do you regret it?"

"I do."

"Well, that makes everything right, does it not?" Robert paced then turned to his father. "Do you ken how I found out?" He shouted, "I met you—in France—when you were younger. You knew it would happen, and you let me go there and meet you face-to-face."

"I did not know what would happen, but yes, I suspected you might."

Robert turned away, shaking his head.

His father stepped around Robert until he was facing him. "If I had told you the truth, would you have gone?"

Robert's eyes flashed to his father's, but he offered no answer, only the bitter sting of emotion that could not be masked.

Brother Thomas said, "I had to make sure that you went."

Robert lifted his chin as he shut his eyes and exhaled. Violet wanted to reach out to him, but she could only watch. He looked as if he had internal bleeding that no one would know of unless they loved him. And she did.

But Brother Thomas's eyes held back pain. She was torn, for she knew Robert's anguish, but she saw Brother Thomas's too.

Robert went to the window and stared into the night sky. "Everything was a lie—who I was, who we were to each other. But one thing was true. I was always alone."

"We would have lost our home." His father put his hand on Robert's shoulder, but Robert pulled free with a jerk of his shoulder.

"Oh, aye. Not to mention the shame it would have brought upon you."

"And on you."

"I was already a bastard. Just in case I forgot, one of the other boys would always remind me. But at least I had my pride and my honor. I knew what was right, and I did it—which is more than I can say for you. For you not only lied to me, but you lied in God's name—robbing graves and passing the bones off as relics with no qualms. Oh, yes, now I have a father. And I am ashamed."

Robert grasped Violet's wrist and pulled her along as he stormed out of the room.

HE LED her all the way to her cell and, making sure no one saw them, went inside and closed the door. Violet had never seen anger like this. His eyes had the same focused energy as when he'd fought off attackers. He moved with the same singular purpose that shut out everything except what he needed to survive. She touched his arm, and he turned, looking almost startled.

"Talk to me," she said.

His eyes bore through her with an anger that made her uneasy. "No. No more talk. No more doing the right thing so people will see that I'm more than a bastard. No more."

Words wouldn't help him, yet she felt compelled to say something. "I'm so sorry."

He shook his head and turned toward the door. He stopped there, leaned his arm on the door, and buried his face in his elbow. Nearly silent, he stayed there as minutes went by.

She put a hand on his shoulder. "If I could, I would take the pain for you."

He turned to her with red eyes. "I believe that you would."

Violet slipped her arms about him and laid her head on his chest.

"Oh, my love." He held her head, rested his cheek on the top of her head, and sighed. "I'm so weary of doing what's right, and I'm weary of being alone."

He touched his lips to her forehead. It was a small kiss, like a spark that floats up from a fire and is gone in the darkness. But this spark landed and burned. Robert clutched at her shoulders and slid his palm down to grasp thick folds of cloth, tugging at any clothing that got in his way. Layer by layer, he unlaced and freed her while she unfastened his doublet and pulled off his clothing until skin was bared to meet skin. In the stark cell—naked, trusting, and driven by need—they joined their warm bodies, hiding their longing and bliss in hushed sighs and moans until they lay spent and entwined. Content to drift off to sleep, they left pain and sorrow outside, where it would wait until morning.

A LOUD RAP at the door woke them. Violet called out, "I'll need a few moments."

Through the door, shuffling feet and unintelligible murmurs grew fainter. When both were dressed, Violet pressed her ear to the door. Moments passed with no sound from outside. She faced Robert, who was standing behind her. Taking hold of his doublet, she pulled him against her and breathed in his scent.

He leaned against her, pressing her back to the door, and quietly moaned in her ear. "Dinnae tempt me." He proceeded to tempt her with a languorous kiss.

With a bracing breath, Violet gently pushed him away until he took a reluctant step backward. She slipped through the door first and watched as black robes disappeared around the corner. She tapped the door, and Robert slipped out of her cell unobserved. Together, they rounded the corner and walked along the corridor.

One of the monks saw them and rushed to Robert. "Come, Brother Thomas is ill. He's been asking for you."

Robert hesitated, but Violet gripped his arm and urged him along until they arrived at Thomas's cell. Several monks unwittingly blocked the doorway, but when they saw Robert, they parted. Violet followed Robert with her hand in his. Brother Thomas lay in bed with a pale sheen on his face. Robert sat in the chair by his cot. Thomas curled his fingers over Robert's sleeve as if trying to tug it. His lips moved a bit, but no sound came out. Robert bent over and brought his ear closer.

His father looked up with searching eyes. "I'm sorry."

Robert's eyebrows drew together. A moment passed,

during which Violet thought she might reach out to do what Robert could not. But Robert put his hand over his father's and gripped it tightly. Blinding tears filled her eyes, and she knew little more than the fact that the son had returned to his father and put aside whatever lay between them. In that moment, love for Robert rooted itself so deeply within her that Violet would no longer feel whole without him.

A WEEK LATER, Brother Thomas could manage a few steps with assistance, but he quickly grew tired. Outside, he sat and lifted his face to the sun. "We must enjoy days such as this, for we don't know when the next one will be."

Robert saw Violet seated on one side of his father, and he sat down on the other. The birds were in full-throated song on that glorious day.

Brother Thomas leaned back against the bench and took several uneasy breaths. "After we arrived here, the abbot guessed Claudine's secret. With no choice, she confirmed his suspicion that she was with child, explaining that she had confessed her sin and been cast out of her convent in Paris. She arrived in Laon, where I took pity upon her and escorted her here, hoping that she would find mercy and perhaps a new home. The abbot could have cast her out, but he did not. We took that as a sign of his mercy and, perhaps, of God's forgiveness."

Robert leaned his elbows on his knees and absently played with the petals of a wild flower he had picked.

Brother Thomas went on. "For a time, life was quiet

and good. If anyone saw through our story, they did not voice their suspicions. We were drawn into the rhythm of life here."

Robert watched the breeze stir the leaves of a nearby tree.

Violet spoke, shaking her head. "Didn't you ever want to go away and live on your own like a family instead of keeping your secret?"

"How? We had nothing—no money, no property. Even if we could have managed, what would happen when the baby was born? We had to think of what was best for the child. We would have a home where we could watch Robert grow, and he would be raised and educated for a life we could never have given him. Claudine wished that for him. How could I deny her?"

Robert crumbled the flower and watched the petals fall to the ground. "Could you not have told me that you were my father? Perhaps not when I was young, but what stopped you when I was grown?"

Brother Thomas's forehead was lined with regret. "After lying for so many years, I couldn't bring myself to tell you the truth."

"Everyone knew I was a bastard. I'd heard it often enough. How could this be worse?"

"Children are cruel," Brother Thomas said, looking off into the distance. Slowly, he shook his head. "No, you were better off not knowing."

Robert slammed his hand on the bench and leapt to his feet. "Och! Dinnae tell me that you were protecting me."

His father took in a ragged breath. "I was protecting her memory. Raising questions would have served no purpose except to make things worse by dragging her name through the mud a second time. It would have dishonored her and you as well." His breathing grew increasingly labored, drawing Violet's concern.

She laid her hand on his shoulder. "Brother Thomas, let's go inside and rest."

He smiled at her. "You're too kind."

A warm smile bloomed on her face. "You're the first to see that in me."

"I can't understand why. Are the men in your time so unobservant?"

Violet lifted an eyebrow. "They have different priorities for what they choose to observe."

"Then they're fools."

Violet tilted her head in agreement and started to smile, but Brother Thomas winced and faltered. Robert lunged toward his father and caught him, then he slipped an arm about Thomas's back for support. Robert's eyes met Violet's, sharing a look of concern. Thomas winced and bent over, clutching his chest, while his other hand gripped Robert's arm. Robert lifted his father to his feet, but Thomas sank to the bench. Violet called out for help.

Through his pain, Brother Thomas struggled to speak, "The abbot."

HE NEVER REGAINED CONSCIOUSNESS. His dying words were for the abbot, so the abbot was summoned from Edinburgh to bury him. Without hesitation, the abbot agreed, which gave Robert a measure of comfort.

The day after Brother Thomas was buried, Robert sat

outside with Violet on the same bench where the three of them had last spoken.

Violet watched some monks make their way through the cloisters. "Everyone thought so highly of him."

"Except his own son. He thought I despised him." Robert made sure his face revealed no sign of the guilt that tormented him. "I held him to an impossible standard, and now it's too late."

Violet turned toward him. "Too late for what?"

"To tell him I forgive him." He swallowed and looked away. "That he was always a father to me. I loved him like one."

Violet slipped her hand into his, and they sat in silence until evening shadows stretched over the grass from the trees.

Within days, Robert had come to know both his mother and father as they once were when they were young. Having known them was a gift, but their loss followed too quickly after. Now he was alone and adrift, which wasn't a new feeling. He had felt it in varying degrees for most of his life, so returning to that state should have been easy. It was not.

The next morning, the abbot found Robert outside, walking alone in the garden before Violet was up.

"May I speak with you?" the abbot asked.

"Aye," Robert answered.

"Come to my office when you're finished here." Without waiting for an answer, the abbot walked away.

Robert watched as he happened upon some of the monks and shared a few words with them. After, he cast a sharp look back at Robert and rounded the corner.

CHAPTER 13

THE OFFER

Robert took a seat in the office Father Abbot was using while he was in Perth. The abbot seemed far more inclined to engage in light conversation than Robert, who was too caught up in his personal grief to contribute to any discussion. Besides which, it felt strange to be with him after seeing him in the past. That visit had been brief enough that the abbot was unlikely to remember it, but it had not been years for Robert. He would have to be careful not to let anything slip that might betray him or invite questions he could not easily answer. Thus on his guard, Robert remained aloof and gave the appearance of manners, waiting until he could retreat to his cell.

Robert looked up to find Father Abbot peering expectantly at him. He had missed something. "I'm sorry. I didn't—"

The abbot offered a sympathetic smile. "'Tis not a bad life here, is it?"

"No, I've had far better life than most, and I'm

grateful for it." He met the abbot's steady gaze, but something flickered in the abbot's eyes. It was gone before Robert could decipher it.

The abbot rested his arms on the desk and leaned forward. "I'd like you to think about something." He looked at Robert with a crooked smile. "We're in need of someone like you in Edinburgh."

Robert smiled. "Do you mean as a monk?"

"Aye, I do."

Robert shook his head. "I once thought I might go down that road, but I'm led in another direction."

"The lass?"

"Aye."

"So you love her?"

"I do."

Father Abbot pushed back from the desk and stood. "Very well, then. As you've made your decision, I wish you well."

"Thank you, Father Abbot."

With little more said, Robert was on his way back to Violet. He couldn't help but feel that there had been more to their short conversation than Robert could grasp. He exhaled. He was too caught up in the events and emotions of the past few days. He would think more clearly after some sleep.

Robert's thoughts strayed to Violet. They hadn't slept together since before Brother Thomas had died. Robert had withdrawn into his own grief and guilt. Violet had been by his side through it all, but he had been barely aware of his own actions, let alone hers. He found himself wanting her near to make plans for a future—their future. But what would that be, not to mention where or when?

He lingered in the hall outside Violet's cell while two monks carried on a long conversation nearby. To avoid looking obvious, Robert walked along and disappeared around a corner, where he stood and waited for what seemed like an eternity. After they had gone, Robert tapped on Violet's door.

She opened it and stood with her hand on the door. "Is it time for supper already?"

He looked to either side to make sure no one was about, then he guided her by the waist back inside and closed the door behind him. Violet's eyes shone as he bent to kiss her. He pulled her against him and kissed her with renewed fervor.

"We havenae talked of the future."

She rested her hands on his shoulders. "We've had quite a bit going on." She peered at him more closely. "Are you all right?"

That drew a bright smile from him. "Aye, for a man who's in love."

A smile lit her eyes. "What did Father Abbot say?"

"'Tis not what he said, but what I realized while he was talking to me."

"Robert, you're not making sense."

He grinned. "No, I suppose I'm not." He grasped her hands and drew her close to him. "I want to be with you—wherever, whenever we can. I would like you to promise to be mine, and I make that same promise to you." He looked worried while awaiting her answer.

Seeing his worry, she smiled and touched his cheek and his mouth then kissed him.

"And?" He looked thoroughly frustrated.

With a light laugh, she answered, "You know that I will."

The fact that she persisted in smiling didn't help matters any. "I know no such thing."

She said, "You do now, because I just told you I will. I'll go anywhere you go. How could you even doubt it?"

"Because I've never felt I belonged anywhere, but I feel it with you."

Violet nodded. "I know."

"But you're smiling. Do you find me amusing?"

No longer smiling, Violet said, "No. It's just that I love you so much that I wondered how you could feel the same about me."

"Oh, lass, you cannae imagine how much." He gave up trying to speak. Instead his hands claimed the places he longed to feel pressed against him, and his mouth found its way from her lips to her ear. He brought his hands to the edge of her neckline and folded his fingers over the edge. "Take this off now."

A bell rang for vespers. Violet lifted her eyes with a startled expression. Neither moved for a moment.

Robert slid his palms deliberately over her breasts to her waist, and he pulled her against him and let out a frustrated growl. He lifted his face, full of helpless remorse. "They will notice our absence."

Violet sighed. "Then we'd best not be absent."

Robert held her wrists and removed her hands from about his waist. "Dinnae touch me, or I'm likely to cause quite a scandal by keeping you here."

Violet firmly took him by the shoulders and turned him toward the door. "Leave now."

He turned, quietly laughing. "You must go first, as it's your cell. To make sure no one sees me?"

She gasped. "What was I thinking? Do you see what you've done to me?"

"Not nearly enough. But I'd gladly remedy that."

Violet opened the door and slipped out before he made good on his offer.

AFTER SUPPER, they made a discreet escape and went for a walk, their way lit by the summer moon's glow.

Robert stopped under a shadowy ash tree and took her hand. "There's one thing we haven't discussed."

She said playfully, "Oh, I think there might be more than one."

Robert was too deep in thought to give in to her mood. "We must decide where to live, and by where, I mean when."

"I've learned not to plan too far ahead."

"We'll want to get married."

Violet smiled. "I suppose."

He hooked his arm about her waist and yanked her against him. "You suppose?"

Violet laughed.

Robert leaned closer until his lips brushed hers. "I'll not marry a lass who supposes. Do you want me or not?"

Her smile faded. "Yes."

"How much?" He lowered his chin and peered into her eyes.

"Enough," she without hesitation.

"Just enough?" He clapped a hand to his heart. "Oh, my love, you pierce my heart with such declarations!"

With a crooked smile, she nodded. "Enough to marry you wherever or whenever you'll have me." What began as light amusement did not end so. "All I want is you."

A moment passed, and the world about them drew to a hush, as if it knew better than to shatter the stillness between them.

"And what do you want?" she asked.

He leaned back and looked at the night sky. "I want to belong. I dinnae care where, but I want that for us and for our family. We must have a place that is ours, where our children will grow and have a home." He looked at her intently.

Violet lifted her chin and looked into his eyes. "I want that too."

Content, as if that were all that could lie in their path, Robert held her face and kissed her.

THEY HAD WONDERED and dreamed then given up talking. But somehow by morning, they had fashioned a plan for their future together. Together, they stood at the abbot's door.

When Father Abbot opened the door, Robert said, "We came to wish you farewell. Violet and I are to be married. We're leaving to go to her home." He left out the part about how her home was in the twenty-first century and the fact that she was not Catholic. He wasn't quite sure which the abbot would find more disturbing, so he chose not to find out.

"Leaving? When?"

Robert grinned. "Well, now actually." Seeing the abbot's surprise, he added, "We've no reason to tarry."

The abbot's brow furrowed. "Of course not." A broad smile lit his face as he turned to Violet and clasped her hand in both of his. "I wish you both happiness."

"Thank you, Father Abbot."

Robert caught himself staring. He couldn't get enough of her smile and the way her eyes shone with its warmth.

Minutes later, they closed the abbot's door and walked through the cloisters for the last time. As they reached the stable, brooding clouds rolled in on a threatening wind. Young Will, the lad from the stable, rode with them to the foot of Kinnoull Hill, where he tethered their horse to his and rode back to the friary. They swore him to secrecy, for no one embarking on a journey from Perth would be left at the hill without someone wondering why. After they bade Will farewell, they began their climb to the cave. They would go live in Violet's home for a time, as she had in his, then they would decide where their future would be. They would be there together, and that was enough.

A storm tossed leaves and whipped branches about as they worked their way up the hill toward the cave. Robert stayed close behind Violet. When he saw her hand tremble, he touched her back to remind her that he was there beside her. It started to rain, and the dirt path grew muddy and slick. Robert worried about Violet's skirts growing heavier as the rain soaked through them. The path leveled out for a few steps.

Violet stopped and clung to a small tree trunk that

seemed to grow out of the rocks. "I'm sorry. I just need a minute."

"I'm here. Take your time."

Violet leaned her face into her hands, but Robert knew she was crying. He held on to the tree with one hand and circled her waist with the other. "It's all right. I've got you, and I will not let go."

With a nervous laugh, Violet said, "So we'll fall together?"

Robert tightened his arm. "No. We'll not fall. Look at me and say it."

She looked boldly into his eyes. "No."

He wouldn't relent. "And the rest?"

Weakly, she said, "We'll not fall."

"There's a good lass."

Whenever he said that, she winced. With one last skeptical glance at Robert, she took a deep breath and proceeded to take a few steps then some more.

When at last they reached the cave, Violet went straight to the back.

Robert followed, swept her into his arms, and planted a kiss that he hoped might be sufficient reward for the climb. "I love you even more now than I did at the bottom of the hill."

With an uncomfortable frown, Violet said, "Do you? Well, that's enough love for me."

Robert laughed. "You dinnae have to climb cliffs to earn my love."

Violet let out a huge sigh. "Well, that's good, 'cause as much as I love you, if that's what it costs, then I might have to settle for less."

He shook his head. "You'll not have to. My love knows no bounds."

The corner of her mouth turned up. "I could get used to this. I wonder when it was that men lost this fine art of flattery? I like it. I don't even mind if it's false."

Robert's eyes flared. "False? Oh, lass, if you dinnae believe me, how can I convince you?"

He pressed his mouth to hers. Outside the wind blew, but neither cared, for their love was stronger.

CHAPTER 14
THE AWAKENING

The unmistakable sound of a wheel-lock pistol being cocked woke Robert. He carefully lifted his hands and focused wary eyes on the man barely visible in the gray mist of pre-dawn.

Violet stirred. "Father Abbot?"

She began to sit up, but her sudden movement startled the abbot, and he pointed his pistol at her.

"The young lovers. How sweet." The abbot regarded them with a wistful smile while he kept his pistol pointed at Violet. "Robert, first lay your weapons on the ground before you. If you do anything foolish, I'll shoot her."

Robert set his sword and dirk in front of the abbot's feet.

"And the sgian dubh."

Robert's eyes narrowed as he pulled the sgian dubh from his boot. "Whatever brought you here concerns me alone. You've no business with Violet."

Ignoring him, the abbot said, "Now stand and lift your arms, and slowly step back."

Robert did as he was told while keeping a suspicious eye on the abbot.

The abbot pointed the gun at Robert and said to Violet, "Now it's your turn. Give me any weapons you've got." Violet opened her mouth to protest, but the abbot said, "If I find one, I'll use it on you."

Robert said, "Give it to him."

Violet lay the dirk on the ground then returned to Robert's side. Something in Robert's demeanor drew a smile from the abbot. "I recall love like that burning so bright that I feared it would consume me."

"Who was she?" Robert asked, stalling until he could determine what was the best thing to do. When he got no response, Robert quietly said, "Father Abbot?"

"Hmm? Oh, who was she? What does it matter? She's gone."

"But she meant something to you."

The abbot nodded and looked at Robert for a long while. "And to you. You look like her. No one saw anything of your father in you, so they never suspected, the fools. They arrived together, and she later turned out to be with child. The monks saw the best, because that was what they wanted to believe, but I saw the truth."

Robert's mind raced as he tried to understand how his parents' past related to the gun pointed at him.

The abbot went on. "And I saw them. I followed them once on a late summer's day. They walked into the fields. The wind stirred the barley so they didn't hear me approach until it was too late. I'd never seen such beauty. Lying there, with the grain fanning about her and framing her beauty in gold. She was transcendent."

Robert knocked the gun out of the abbot's hand.

They grappled, but the abbot fought back with maneuvers that took Robert by surprise. He fought like the Jesuit priests who had attacked them, kicking and slicing with swift moves that caught Robert off guard. Without a weapon, Robert was barely a match for such tactics. Within minutes, the abbot had his hand clamped about Robert's neck as he pinned him to the ground.

Smiling over his easy victory, the abbot said, "Your father provided me with an income for years, so devoted was he to protecting her memory. He had a true gift for creating relics."

Robert thought of the disdain he had heaped upon his father over making false relics. All the while, he was being blackmailed by the abbot.

The abbot sighed. "Ah, well, as much as I'd like to reminisce, I've a busy day ahead."

"Don't let us keep you," Violet muttered.

"Aye, well, you've kept us quite busy. But alas, I've grown weary of chasing you two over the countryside—or rather, my men have."

"You're one of them." Robert saw from the abbot's reaction that he knew to whom Robert referred. All along, the Jesuits who had attacked them were working for the abbot.

The abbot grinned. "We were missionaries together ten years ago in Japan. But the Japanese decided they didn't want to be converted, so we passed the time learning their ways. The Buddhist monks taught us Fujian White Crane Kung Fu. Fascinating, really—as much strength of the mind as the body."

Violet lunged at him, but he moved to the side to avoid her. While she was off balance, he swatted her with a force that sent her backward to the ground. She lay with the wind knocked out of her, unable to move for a moment. With the abbot's attention on Violet, Robert seized the chance to land a blow to the abbot's jaw, then another, before the abbot jabbed his fingertips into Robert's throat. Robert fell, fighting for breath. He recovered first and grasped Violet's hand. She looked at him with such trust that a drive to protect her coursed through him.

"To see you two so in love makes me sorry that I'll have to separate you." The abbot sat halfway between them and the cave's opening, aiming his pistol first at one then the other, as if they needed reminding that he had a gun. "I don't want to hurt either of you. The gun's simply here to remind you to follow instructions."

"Instructions?" Robert asked.

When the rising sun lit the cave with its light, Robert and Violet exchanged uneasy glances. It would soon be too late for their journey.

A curious look crossed the abbot's face as he saw the exchange but said nothing. "First, tell me how it is done." When Robert looked quizzically at him, he added, "Your little trips to the past and the future."

Violet exhaled, aggravated. "Is that what this is about? You want to travel through time? Well, be my guest. Bon voyage!"

Robert gave Violet's hand a cautionary squeeze, prompting a sharp glance from her.

For the first time, the abbot regarded Violet with interest. "She's a bold one."

Violet bristled and scowled.

The abbot smiled at her reaction. "'Tis not such a bad thing, my child. In fact, it could be quite useful."

Robert wasn't sure which of them he was angrier with. He could do nothing about the abbot, but he wished Violet had kept quiet. It wouldn't help their cause for her to allow her emotions to rule unchecked. He could practically hear the abbot forming a plan to take full advantage of her anger, so he tried to distract him. "Why time travel?"

A spark lit the abbot's eyes. "'Tis a wondrous thing to imagine, isn't it?"

Robert made no effort to hide his impatience.

The abbot leaned against the cave wall. "And then there's the scroll. All of those drawings and symbols—but what does it mean?"

Robert shrugged. "I dinnae ken, nor does anyone else."

The abbot went on. "If you look at it, which I did at great length, there are symbols and places that made me wonder if it might not be a means of guiding people to places they might not otherwise know how to find."

Violet squinted. "Like a low-tech GPS?"

Both men turned blank faces toward her.

Violet shook her head and said softly, "Never mind. I guess that would just make it a map."

The abbot said, "Imagine the power of knowing the future and traveling through time to reshape the past. We'd exert limitless influence over the world."

Robert said, "I'm sure that's what the Templars did *not* want."

"Except for themselves. They amassed quite a widespread financial network. Rulers all over Europe were indebted to them. Once you control money, you control those who need it. Oh, they would have gone further, if permitted."

"I don't believe you."

The abbot smiled. "Because your world is small. You can't see the grand realm of options it offers. I do. And that is why I want to know how to travel through time. Only then will we be able to put the scroll to its proper use. But first we'll need the scroll."

Robert scoffed. "It's an old piece of linen with historical value, no doubt, but I dinnae ken what makes you think it has anything to do with time travel—or maps, for that matter."

The abbot nodded. "For a long time, I did not. I thought that the scroll itself held all of the answers. But I realized it did not—and I thank you for that—when you appeared with this lovely young woman, with her strange speech and ways. It was almost as if she were from the future. Then there were your parents. After they arrived, my men found a Templar tunic at the foot of Kinnoull Hill. When by chance I caught a glimpse of the scroll, the pieces began to take shape. Strange people from the past and the future, and a scroll with strange markings—and all connected to one man: your father."

Robert glared at the abbot but held his tongue.

"And to think, I'd nearly sent him away. He had far overstayed his welcome and showed far too much interest in your mother. But when I caught him trying to leave with the wee child, I was certain that he was the father. Once I'd figured that out, it was easy to keep him from leaving. I made a bargain with him. He could stay at the monastery with you if he became a monk and made relics to give to our benefactors in exchange for their generous donations, which did not always go to the church. I made money and waited for some small crack in his armor that might lead me to the scroll. It had disappeared, but I was sure that he had it. It was only a matter of time before it turned up. And it has.

"And now here you are, ready to help me." The abbot looked at Robert as though this were no more than a routine daily matter. "Enough talk. Get up, both of you."

Robert reached out to help Violet to her feet. Still vexed, she refused his assistance and stood on her own—until her foot caught on her skirts. She had to grab Robert's arm to steady herself. But instead of standing beside him as he expected, she stepped toward the abbot, who thrust his pistol toward her.

Robert was fuming but managed to speak in a hush, "Stay beside me, lass. That's an order."

Violet gasped and made little effort to keep her voice down. "An order? Well, who could argue with that?" Refusing to engage in further discussion with Robert, she turned to the abbot. "Look, Father Abbot, I can see you're upset. If you'll just take a moment—and maybe put down the gun—I'm sure we could find some common ground here."

The abbot looked at Robert with a grimace. "If you love her, you'll silence her now."

Robert shrugged and shook his head. "I cannae do that, but if you'll stay by the side of the cave over there, we can send the lass home."

Violet planted her feet shoulder distance apart and stood her ground. "The lass isn't going home, so you can both disabuse yourselves of that notion."

The abbot took her refusal far better than Robert did. He was furious. Had he made a mistake in thinking he could grow used to her modern ways? Perhaps they were simply too different. But he loved her. He would have felt more at ease sending her home to safety, but if she was determined to stay, then he was equally determined to find a way through this. "You heard the lass. She isn't going home."

Violet turned to him, looking both stunned and pleased.

"It matters little to me what she does," the abbot said.

"Good, then shall we proceed?"

The abbot lowered the gun and slid it under his belt. "Don't give me cause to take it back out, for I'll shoot you both with no further thought."

Robert nodded.

The abbot said, "I want to go back."

"If this is about my mother, I'll not take you there."

"Your mother? No. Oh, I did love her, but she didn't share my feelings. And I was a priest, after all. How could she have been part of God's plan?"

"Oh—and pointing that gun at us is?" Violet rolled her eyes.

She might have gone on, but Robert squeezed her hand again, which by now must have had indents from his fingers on it—not that it kept her from talking. His fear was that without meaning to, she might provoke the abbot into doing something violent.

The abbot said, "Since you posed the question, the answer is yes. If what my men and I do furthers God's purpose, then what we do is God's work."

Robert tried not to glare at him. "So chasing us out of

Perth, killing Henry, the attack on the bridge, and at the castle—that was all God's work?"

"Aye."

"God's been busy," Violet said dryly as she leaned against the cave wall.

"If only you had handed the scroll over, we would have been done with all of this." The abbot glanced outside at the sun masked by thick morning mist.

With narrowing eyes, Robert watched him. "But it was under your nose all those years. Why bother now?"

"I didn't know about it until you brought it to me."

"You could have taken it then."

The abbot shook his head. "No, you would have caused a stir and made things uncomfortable for us."

"Uncomfortable?" Robert thought of how uncomfortable he and Violet had been when they were being chased over the countryside and attacked by the abbot's men.

"I wasn't about to let a hasty decision spoil years of work. We have kept our sect a secret while we waited for the chance to accomplish our goal."

"Which is?" Robert's brow creased.

"Returning the Church to power."

Robert said, "The church that would have killed my father, given the chance? Or have you forgotten my father was a Templar?"

"Aye, he was. And he carried one of their secrets, which he passed on to you. Which brings us to you."

Robert tried not to scoff. "I've nothing for you."

The abbot tilted his head and smiled. "But you do. First we'll get the scroll, then you'll tell me what you ken about how to travel through time."

Robert frowned. "I dinnae ken how it works."

"But you ken how to do it. The map is no good without that."

"Time travel is not without peril." As he spoke, sunlight shone into the cave. Robert glanced outside. The mist was clearing, and a gap in the clouds brought the sunlight they needed to travel. But more clouds threaten to block it again.

The abbot paced. "I don't need a lecture from you about the perils. I need you to take me to the scroll."

Robert studied the abbot. "But your men have it. They took it from me at Rosslyn Castle."

The abbot frowned in confusion then opened his mouth to speak, but he appeared to think better of it. Robert wondered at that. Either one or more of the men had run off on their own with the scroll, or he and Violet had altered events when they went back to retrieve it. They hadn't only rescued the scroll, but they had altered its fate.

Seeing doubt in the abbot's eyes, Robert pressed his advantage. "If that's what you were hoping to find here, then I'm afraid we must disappoint you."

"Take me back to the last place and time that you saw it."

Robert shook his head. "We cannae do that."

The abbot paced before Robert. "You can, or you would not be here. Where were you planning to go?"

"Nowhere now. It's too late."

Violet's eyes shot toward the sun, which still shone into the cave. Her glance did not escape the abbot's notice.

His eyes lit with sudden realization. "The sunlight?" He watched her reaction. "That's it, isn't it?"

Violet looked at Robert, her eyes full of regret.

Robert turned his attention to the abbot. "If that's all this is about, we'll not stop you. You're here, so you must ken what to do."

"I saw Brother Thomas and Sister Claudine coming out of the cave once. I've tried to change times, but it didn't work for me."

Robert nodded. "Aye, well, allow me to assist you. Nothing would make me happier than to see you disappear."

Anger burned in the abbot's eyes, but he choked it back and kept his attention on Robert, who had what he wanted.

"Stand over here, facing the light." Ignoring Violet's stunned look, Robert indicated a spot in the center. "It's important to find the spot with the most intense light, or it willnae work. Here."

Robert tentatively approached to guide the abbot to the right spot. When the abbot averted his eyes to follow Robert's instructions, Robert struck him on the wrist and knocked the pistol to the ground. But the abbot countered by seizing Violet about the waist. And the two disappeared.

CHAPTER 15

ADRIFT IN TIME

R obert rushed to the spot where Violet had stood moments ago, but a cloud crossed the path of the sun. He cried out her name—not because he thought she might hear him, but because he knew she would not. He had lost her. She was in some other time, in the past or the future. For all of the abbot's years of working with wealthy patrons, he had learned to read people and how to use them. He had to have known that Robert would never tell him where the scroll was, no matter what torture he might have inflicted. But Violet didn't understand people like the abbot. Jesuits lived by different rules and weren't bound by things like truth and honor. She would try to withstand his coercive tactics for Robert, but that was exactly what Robert didn't want her to do. As he imagined her with the abbot, he wanted only for her to be safe. The scroll, which had once been Robert's sole mission, was no longer important. Violet was everything to him. If he thought it would save her, he would hurl the scroll into the crashing waves from the highest tower of Castle Girnigoe.

Castle Girnigoe. Violet was too clever to fall prey to the abbot. She would try to outsmart him. But how? She would lead Robert to them. Where else could she go and be sure Robert would follow? Castle Girnigoe. She knew Robert would look for her there. Although going there would put the scroll at risk, it would bring them together. After that, they would focus on the scroll. No other place made as much sense. All he needed to do was to find a way to get there first, before the abbot and Violet arrived. As the plan took shape, the sun burst through the drifting clouds and shone into the chamber, and Robert was gone.

He awoke in a place that looked unfamiliar. Waves pounded the rocks and sent spray back to the sea. He stood in ankle-deep water and went to the mouth of a cave. No one was about, nor was there a sign that people lived anywhere near. The thought formed that he might have gone back to a time when there were no people, if there was such a time. Before him was the sea, and behind him, rough-edged cliffs stretched skyward. Cut away from the cliffs was a sort of channel that sloped upward. He walked up its path to the top of the cliff, where he paused, unable to believe the sight before him. His father had once told him that destiny played a part in the journey through time. If landing at the very castle he sought wasn't a matter of destiny, then it was uncanny good fortune. But as he drew closer, he saw that the castle, as well as the cliff it rested upon, was in ruins and crumbling into the sea.

Robert cursed as he sank to the ground. "I'm too late."

He buried his face in his hands. He had come to a time in the future, leaving Violet somewhere in the past with the abbot. But where? Until now, they had always arrived close to when they expected. Brother Thomas had told him that time made no mistakes and that people were taken where they needed to be, even if they didn't understand why. If that were true, why was he in the future and not by the side of the woman he loved? How could he help her from here?

He could try to go back, but if he believed Brother Thomas, that was the wrong thing to do. One thing he did know was that the journeys were never exact. He might be a day early or late. If he left, she might arrive the next day. How would he know? If he did leave, he could spend an eternity looking and failing to find her. In the end, he decided to trust that his travels had brought him to the right time and place.

During the days that passed, people arrived in cars like the ones he had seen when he traveled to New York during Violet's time. People walked about what was left of the castle. In secret, he watched them come and go, but Violet wasn't among them. At night, he made camp down by the water. After the visitors left but before darkness fell, Robert went in search of fresh water to drink but found none. From stones that lay about, Robert fashioned a cistern to collect rainwater.

On the third day, he was rewarded with rain. While water collected, he caught some fish and cooked it over a fire beneath the shelter of overhanging rocks. When he ate the fish, along with some plants he had gathered, it felt like a feast. He leaned back against the rocks and, soothed by the warmth of the fire, thought of Violet. He wondered if she were warm and content. He felt strangely connected to her, but he loved her. Why would he not? But rather than find comfort in feeling her presence, he felt deeply troubled. The last time he saw her, she had been in grave danger. He said her name as if the sound of it would bring her to him. It was all he could do, and it wasn't enough.

Awash with the bright light that always blinded her during the journey, Violet felt the abbot's firm grip on her arm. They stumbled and fell onto the floor of the cave. They were in the same place, but what year it was, Violet couldn't have said.

The abbot pulled her to her feet and yanked her toward the cave entrance. "Hurry. We've a scroll to find."

Still disoriented from the journey through time, Violet could think only of how her arm hurt as he pulled her toward the light. When they got to the mouth of the cave, she had to squint into the sun. She glanced back. If she could free herself, she might have a chance of escaping through time and leaving the abbot there. But his grip was too firm. She had seen enough of his martial arts skill to be cautious, if not afraid.

He pushed her forward. "You go first so I can keep an eye fixed on you."

Digging in her heels, she leaned away from him and tugged her wrist back to resist him. "I can't. I'm afraid of heights." While it was true, she had never been quite so dramatic about it.

"Och! You vexatious hellion."

He reached for his pistol, but he had left it behind. Seeing this, Violet turned and put all of her weight into yanking her arm free. The force threw the abbot backward, and he fell. Violet stared at the cave opening, too stunned to think clearly.

Then she heard Robert call to her, like a lost memory. She turned and rushed to a spot on the cave floor that was still bright with sunlight. A gust of wind stirred the leaves. The next moment, she found herself cold and wet, water swirling about as she lay on loose rocks. Pulling herself up, she staggered and grabbed hold of the side of a cliff. She tried to call out, but no sound came. She leaned on the rocks, gathering strength for more steps. She proceeded like that, a few steps at a time, until weariness overcame her, and she sank to the ground.

ROBERT SAT in the tower of the castle and watched clouds drift drowsily over the moon as its broken reflection cast a path over the sea. He had spent five such nights since his arrival with no sign of Violet. While he would never give up searching for her, waiting there wasn't bringing him closer to her. Over the past week, he had thought about what to do next and had planned every step with attention to detail.

Before leaving, he had to leave some sort of sign that he hoped she would find if she came searching for him. So he had roughly etched a scroll in the wall of the time travel cave he had arrived in. He had troubled over how much else to include, since the abbot and his men might also see it. If he wrote down a place, they would follow—providing they knew when to arrive. But that would be a problem with Violet, as well. She might know the right place but not know when to arrive. And that assumed anyone had control over the timing.

Robert thought back on everything they had been through together. Along with nearly every word she had said when they first met, Robert recalled a road she had mentioned. At the time, she had believed she was still near her home on Farmers Mills Road. He wouldn't write the road name in case others saw it and eventually pieced things together, but he was sure she would figure it out from the initials. Because it was part of her life before meeting him, she would also know to go back to her time, where he would find her. So inside the scroll, he scratched FMR.

His plans were made but he was unable to sleep, so he went up to the castle tower for some peace before the next leg of his journey. High above the vast stretches of water and land, he felt removed from his troubles. He dwelled upon how he loved her and further imagined their future together. It had all seemed so impossible in the beginning. They both had their own lives that were so very different —too different to meet one another halfway. He had fought against falling in love with her, even though by the time he was fighting it, he had already fallen. She fell later but put up even more resistance. But love would not be denied. He still didn't know how or when their lives would come together again, but he knew that—if he ever found her—they would. There was no other way he could live.

Robert headed down to his crude camp by the water. Tired but restless, he lay down while the gulls mewed him to sleep. He sat halfway up when a strange sound punctuated the chorus of gulls. They almost sounded human. He lay back down, attributing his reaction to too much time alone.

He was drifting to sleep when he heard it again.

"You're a fool," he said to himself, but he got up and walked toward where the groaning had come from.

The quarter moon shed little light by the shadowy wall of the cliff. He approached a large shape in his path, which turned out to be a large piece of driftwood with a smooth silvery trunk and gnarled branches. He gave it a swift kick for good measure and chastised himself all the way back to camp. He was about to settle back down when, behind him, he heard the faint crunch of footsteps on the stone-covered ground. He pivoted toward the shadowy figure. Whoever was after him ran away, but Robert caught up and tackled his would-be attacker by the waist, throwing both to the ground.

"Och, you're just a wee thing—in skirts," he said. "Lass, what do you think you're doing?"

She took in a sharp breath. "I was looking for you."

Robert loosened his hold. It was too dark to see, but he knew her voice too well. "Violet."

She flung her arms about him and held on to him. She said his name while she touched his lips and face and combed her fingers into his hair.

Robert's arms tensed, and he started to pull himself up. "The abbot—did he follow you?"

"No, he's dead. I didn't mean to—"

"Then you're safe." He pulled her back into his arms. "Promise me—"

"Yes."

He smiled. "You dinnae ken what I was going to say."

"I promise I'll never leave you—unless you want me to. But really, at this point, you've pretty much made a commitment. I know guys don't like that word, but after all we've been through, you owe me."

"Shh..." Robert held her face and put his mouth over hers in a kiss meant to make her forget—about words, about the abbot, and everything else, except what he was determined to say. "Marry me."

Total silence.

Robert frowned and pulled away. Still no answer. "Lass, have you nothing to say?"

"Was that a question? 'Cause it sounded more like an order."

Frustrated, if not fully annoyed, Robert started to speak, but something in her tone stopped him. He touched her cheeks, wet with tears.

She said, "Either way, yes."

They spent the night taking time, for they had all the time in the world, exploring one another with each touch and desire. Time would wait for them while they took each another with a passion that bound them together. After, they made plans and discarded them, laughing and sure that no matter what time held in store for the future, they would travel through it together.

AUTHOR'S NOTE

THANKS TO:

The Retreat, a group of writers who are always there when I need advice, support, laughter, and friendship;

Narrator Jeff Leslie, for sharing his knowledge of Kinnoull Hill and all things Perth-related; and

Author Jacques Antoine, who shared his martial arts knowledge and suggested using Fujian White Crane Kung Fu.

RESEARCH NOTES:

There is an actual scroll housed in a Kirkwall, UK Masonic Lodge. Currently available research does not point toward it containing a map of secret Templar time travel portals. However, no one seems precisely sure what all of those markings mean.

Jesuit missionaries first arrived in Japan in 1543. By that time, knowledge of Fujian White Crane Kung Fu, introduced by Chinese immigrants to Japan in 1392, would have made its way through Japan and thus been available to Jesuit missionaries by the time our fictional Father Abbot and his men were there. They may well have returned home with some martial arts knowledge.

Historically, there seem to have been a number of spellings for the following. In the interest of avoiding confusion, the currently accepted spellings are used in this book: the earldom, the chapel, and the castle are spelled Rosslyn, and the village is spelled Roslin.

Time travel presents interesting paradoxes which, while relevant, are beyond the scope of this novel. This recent editorial from webzine *GeekSnack* highlights some of the issues and explanations I considered while writing *Knight Errant* and *Highland Passage*. Moth, Jason, "Physics 101: Understanding time travel and why we shouldn't dismiss the possibility," GeekSnack, April 20, 2015.

THE HIGHLAND PASSAGE TRILOGY

Highland Passage: Scottish time travel romances (can be read in any order)

THANK YOU!

Thank you for reading! If you enjoyed this book, please consider leaving a review or a rating. Your feedback on bookstore, Goodreads, and Bookbub websites helps other readers discover books they'll enjoy.

BOOK NEWS

Sign up for exclusive updates and offers at
news.jljarvis.com

ABOUT THE AUTHOR

J.L. Jarvis is a left-handed former opera singer/teacher/lawyer who writes books. She now lives and writes on a mountaintop in upstate New York.

jljarvis.com

instagram.com/jljarvis.writer
facebook.com/jljarvis1writer
x.com/JLJarvis_writer
bookbub.com/authors/j-l-jarvis
goodreads.com/jljarvis